Boneset & Feathers

Broken Eye Books is an independent press, here to bring you the odd, strange, and offbeat side of speculative fiction. Our stories tend to blend genres, highlighting the weird and blurring its boundaries with horror, sci-fi, and fantasy.

Support weird. Support indie.

brokeneyebooks.com
twitter.com/brokeneyebooks
facebook.com/brokeneyebooks
instagram.com/brokeneyebooks
patreon.com/brokeneyebooks

Gwendolyn Kiste

BONESET & FEATHERS
by GWENDOLYN KISTE

Published by Broken Eye Books
www.brokeneyebooks.com

Cover illustration by Gawki
Cover design by Scott Gable
Interior design by Scott Gable
Editing by Scott Gable and C. Dombrowski

978-1-940372-57-0 (trade paperback)
978-1-940372-59-4 (hardcover)

Boneset & Feathers

Gwendolyn Kiste

chapter one

When the first crows fall from the sky, the villagers know I'm to blame.

It doesn't take much to guess that it's me, the witch that lives outside of town, the only witch left here. Soon, if the witchfinders keep building their pyres across the countryside, I might be the only witch left anywhere. Then I'll be the one blamed for everything. A failed harvest, a sour business deal, an infant with colic. There will be no ill I can't be punished for.

But even as feathers clog up the villagers' chimneys and talons scrape across the stained-glass windows of the church, I'm none the wiser to it. It's not until I'm halfway to town that I see a crow tumble out of the clouds. At first, I'm sure it's only my eyes playing tricks on me again, a mirage dancing alongside the demons and ghosts that have been pinwheeling at the edges of my vision for years.

So I ignore the harbinger and keep going until it's too late to easily turn back. By the time the crow is joined by starlings and bluebirds and cardinals, all the colors banding across the slate-gray sky of February like a deranged aurora borealis, I'm already at the crossroads, halfway between everywhere and nowhere. With four directions to go and none of them very welcoming, I have only bad choices.

North toward a place I hope never to visit. The capital city that will burn any witch they can get ahold of.

Off the beaten path toward the east and into the Hyland Forest with its ancient phantoms and toadstool circles. I can't help but shudder. These days, some land is too haunted even for a witch.

South toward my spartan cottage, back the way I came, into the quieter woods where I dwell, where one day if I'm lucky, I'll die alone. (If I'm not lucky, I'll die the same way as the others, among flame and straw and screams that go unanswered.)

Or I could grit my teeth and go to the place I've been heading all along, ever since I set out at sunrise this morning. West into the town that doesn't want a witch but is cursed with me anyhow.

The trees murmur all around me, and I hold perfectly still at the crossroads, already knowing what I should do. Turn and race back home as fast as I can, anything to escape this place and these birds. But I only shake my head. That won't work either. After all, if I ran every time I was scared, I'd never stop running.

Two things. That's all I need in the village. Then I might make it until spring thaw.

I clasp my hands in front of me and walk on toward the village.

When I reach the town square, the birds are still falling, and there's no one on the street. They're all hiding inside. Families gather at their front windows, sobbing at the sky, glaring at me as I pass. I tip my head to the ground, a scream blossoming in my throat.

"I didn't do this," I want to tell them, and it's mostly true. This isn't from a spell I cast, but I know they blame me anyhow. They believe my magic has run wild from this grief I can't contain. The same grief the villagers live with too. They have to see the evidence of it every day in the town square where the ground is still charred black from the pyres. It seems no matter how many rainstorms we get, nothing will wash this town clean again. It's been five years since the witchfinders were here, but they more than left their mark.

Wherever you were in the village, you'd know when those men from the capital arrived, their cloaks so thick and billowy they seemed to cover all the rooftops, their boots perfectly polished so that when they loomed over you, you couldn't even look down to escape—you'd only see yourself reflected back in the accusing leather sheen. They roamed our streets, day and night, taking notes in their ledgers, arresting without warrants, shooting our wrens and cardinals and robins out of the sky until they'd chased them all away. Thanks to those men, no one had seen a single bird in this village for five years. That is, until today.

Now the birds cascade around me, and I freeze up in the middle of the street, still wanting to flee back to the forest. The copper rooftop on the corner glimmers in the sun, and I realize I'm already here. The general store, my first stop.

The heavy wooden door swings open in my hand, and I slip inside only to discover it's no safer. What I need is in the back of the store, but that's where everyone else is too, huddled together, tangled up in a human rat king, a smattering of patrons cowering as far from the front window and the carnage as they can get.

I halt in the aisle, only a few paces away, as they stare at me.

"Why is she doing this?" they mumble to each other, their skin wan, their eyes swirling dark. I stay put, not wanting to spook them. If I move too quickly, they might panic en masse, and things will get so much worse.

"Are you open?" I say, and someone lets out a strident laugh. It's the clerk, half-hidden in the far back.

"Why bother asking?" she says. "You'll do whatever you want anyway."

My throat constricts, and I want to tell her how that isn't true, but it won't matter. I might not have done this on purpose, but they'll never believe that because they never believe me.

The clerk slides out from behind the counter, pushing to the front of the crowd. She looks right at me, and I recognize her from years ago, from a different life when I used to teach her and the other girls our age a bit of my hand-me-down magic. How to conjure a glamour, how to see the face of your true love in the runny whites of an egg. I wanted to teach them more, I wanted to teach them everything, but all the parents found out first, and that was that. Mothers and fathers always put a stop to things they don't understand.

"Why do you want to help those girls?" my own mother asked me when she caught me in the forest with them, a ring of salt around us.

"Because they're my friends," I said, and she flashed me a cruel smile that could have stopped time.

"Wait until you need them," she said. "Wait and see how fast they run."

Above us, a bird thuds against the roof, and another and another after that, and the clerk edges closer to me, her jaw set. "Take whatever you need," she says, her voice sharp and cold as chiseled iron.

My head down, I move past the bins of coffee and sugar and spiced tobacco. The aisles are cramped and grimy, and the others watch me as I pass, inching back several steps, terrified they might accidentally brush against me.

"She looks worse," they whisper, and I know they're right. Since the last time I was here in the fall, I've been wasting away, bit by bit. Acorn flour, roasted pine bark, bits of crystallized honey—there isn't much left in my cupboard this time of year, which means there isn't much left of me. But I never come to the village and ask for a meal. I don't trust what they'd put in my food.

The clerk is the only one who comes closer, matching me step for step, tracking me whatever aisle I choose. I breathe in, not remembering what to call her. I used to know her name. I used to know all the girls' names, but like everything about this village, I've done my best to forget. It's easier that way, pretending I never knew her at all.

As I push to the end of the aisle, she drifts one step nearer, cornering me between dusty bins of marjoram and cardamom and cayenne.

"Why do you keep doing this?" The question simmers on her lips, her breath hot and sweet like candied cinnamon. "Why don't you stay gone?"

She glares right through me, her mouth twisted, and I'm sure she's about to scream or spit at me. But then something in her shifts, her face going dark.

"Please, Odette," she says, her eyes glistening, thin tears streaking down her cheeks. "Haven't we lost enough already?"

As if I'm to blame for all this loss instead of the witchfinders.

She thinks it's so simple. All the villagers do. That if I stop doing magic, we'll be safe, and the witchfinders will forget about us.

What no one understands is that I have tried. Every night, I turn away from the dark and do my best to forget. My mind going gray as I erase the spells I memorized as a child, the intricate rituals my mother taught me, those words that can carry the weight of the world in only a few syllables. Over and over, I practice being someone else since being me has done no good.

Except the truth has a terrible tendency of leaking in at the edges. You can only hide from yourself for so long.

On the bottom shelf, I finally spot it. An overstuffed satchel of salt. First item off my list—and one step closer to escaping this town. I reach out for it, but instantly, a sharp murmur jolts through the whole store.

"Your hands," the clerk says, and dread clenches in my guts because I see it too.

My fingernails are caked thick with dirt.

"She's been digging in the cemetery again," the others whisper, and they're right. I'd hoped it was only a bad dream, but these scratches on my palms are real too, from the rusted coffin nails biting into my skin. I was really there last night among the tombs of the other witches. The tombs of my family.

The front window bows inward, and another crow cascades past the front awning. My head spins as I carry the salt to the counter, clasping it close to my chest to keep my hands from trembling, all this power bubbling up inside me. The clerk doesn't bother to meet me. With graveyard dirt on my hands, nobody will come near me now, so I drop my coins on the counter, two pence too many. At least that way, no one can call me a thief.

Back on the street, I dodge down an alley, away from the villagers' prying eyes. A sparrow topples to the cobblestone next to me, followed by a robin and a starling. Together, they look so unreal, their eyes glazed, their bodies still. All the birds are silent. Even as they fall, they make no sound.

I bury my face against the canvas bag, sobbing into the salt, wishing I could help the birds, wishing I'd never come here at all. So long as I stay tucked inside my cottage, nobody will bother me, not even the witchfinders. There are rumors of what haunts the woods, things so much worse than witches. The same things that live in the edges of my vision, swimming there in the dark. That's why I'm here—for this salt. A ring of it around my cottage will seal them out. Then maybe I won't spend tonight in the graveyard again, digging there because the phantoms tell me to.

I lean against the stone wall of the alley to steady myself. One more item—and this day, this trip, will be over. And the place I need is so close, only a few dozen paces to the end of this street. To the seamstress's shop.

It's a small brick house with one room, no windows, and a front door that's always unlocked, always welcoming. Inside, Beatrix hunches over yards of muslin and linen, her world-worn eyes squinting at unraveled hems, her sun-spotted hands smoothing out a fresh seam. She barely glances up from her treadle as the door slams shut behind me.

"Hello, Odette," she says, her voice warm as fresh gingerbread, and I exhale a breath I didn't know I was holding.

Beatrix has never been like the others. For years, she used to practice a bit of folk magic herself. Homemade salves and tinctures and oxymels. How to deliver a stubborn baby, how to break the meanest of fevers. Now she pretends to know only about burlap and spindles and how to sharpen a dull sewing needle. It's safer that way. It's always safer not to be a witch.

"What can I do for you today?" she asks, and I hesitate, my nervous fingers fumbling with a row of buttons and golden clasps and a spool of black thread.

"One yard of red ribbon please," I say, my voice steady, trying not to give myself away.

But Beatrix knows me too well. Her eyes flick up at me. "For a knot spell?" she asks, and when I fidget, saying nothing else, that more than answers her question.

Only it's not for a spell, not really. More like a compulsion. Every time in the night when my fingers start to shake, when my hands remember what it's like to hold an athame or light a taper candle at midnight, I keep myself occupied by tying a knot. This is what I've been doing for years now. Looping every yard of ribbon a hundred times, a thousand even, until my last pieces frayed and crumbled into dust.

That's not exactly magic. If anything, it's the inverse of magic, a world without spells and without power. Just how the villagers want this place.

"Let me see what I've got," Beatrix says. Humming to herself, she roots through a box of jumbled notions, picking out this and discarding that, until finally she tugs a thin bolt of red ribbon from the bunch. Her body hunched, she works slowly, slower than she used to, her hands gnarling like willow roots. She's the same age as my mother, or at least the age my mother would have been. It's strange to think how much older the world is getting.

With a snick-snack of scissors, she cuts an arm's length of ribbon and slides it across the counter to me.

I don't move to take it. "How much do I owe you?" I ask, my hand in my pocket, gripping the last coin to my name.

Beatrix gives me that smile of hers that never seems to fade. "You keep your money, darling. You know that."

I take the ribbon and tuck it in the pocket of my goatskin jacket, nodding goodbye to her. Above us, there's the patter of what sounds like rain, and I wonder which birds are descending on us now.

"Try not to worry, Odette," Beatrix says as I head toward the door. "This storm won't last forever."

Outside, I gaze down the street, the storefronts and houses contorting in size, the whole world moving nearer and farther at the same time. Nearby, a starling hits a slate roof and tumbles into the gutter. Dust and feathers rise up around me along with the wet metallic scent of blood, and my flesh prickles, the sack of salt weighing heavy in my hands. I've got what I came for. It's time to go home. But the quickest way out of town is straight down the street in front of me, the street where I used to live. And I won't look at what's become of the place I called home.

Instead, I take the long way around, past the tavern with its pitched roof and the blacksmith's shop where the furnace is always glowing the color of hellfire. I'm almost to the end of the lane when the stable with its narrow field comes into view. Most of the horses have been herded inside the barn, but a lone palfrey stands against the fence, his liquid eyes staring out into the village, seeing everything and nothing, unperturbed at the falling birds. I reach out and run my fingers through his mane, thick and tangled like briars. The horse isn't like all the villagers. He doesn't cringe at my touch.

But the moment doesn't last. A hulking figure emerges from the stable, his calloused hands with a riding crop always at the ready. He spots me immediately, his face flaring crimson.

"Get out of here, Odette."

I force a smile. "Hello to you too, Samuel."

"I mean it," he says, and a dove topples into a nearby water trough. "You've got no reason to be here."

Next to me, the horse grunts as if in agreement, and I flinch and start walking along the fence, pretending not to notice the white feathers floating like fresh snow through the air.

On the other side, Samuel keeps pace with me, his hand tightening around the riding crop. "Do you think it's wise to stand so close to the fence?"

I smile again. "Do you think it's wise to threaten a witch?"

At this, he exhales a rueful laugh. "You never change, Odette."

"Neither do you, Samuel."

His house is right next door to the stable, a stout little cottage with a tuft of smoke like spun sugar, rising out of the chimney. Behind the front window, there's a flutter of movement, and I seize up, waiting to see a face, waiting to see her. I almost speak her name aloud, the one name I can never forget.

Anna, Samuel's daughter. After the parents dragged all the other girls home, it was only me and her, dancing barefoot around midnight bonfires together. The two of us would creep out our bedroom windows and meet on the street in front of my house.

"Come on," I'd say and lead her by the hand up into the forest. "And don't listen when the wind whispers lies in your ear."

Wherever I went, she'd always giggle and keep up with me. The only one I thought for sure would stick with me forever, and I haven't spoken to her since the night the witchfinders arrested me. That was the way Samuel wanted it, no doubt.

"It's not safe out in those woods," he'd tell Anna, and apparently she finally believed him.

I continue walking, Samuel's eyes still fixed on me. At the end of the fence, I try to break away, but with a swift hand, he opens the gate and crosses in front of me, his broad body blocking my way.

"They're gone for now," he says through clenched teeth. "Don't give those men a reason to return."

I back away, my fingers curling into fists, the satchel of salt contorting in my arms. "I'm not the reason they came in the first place."

"No," he says, "but you'll be the reason they come back."

These words twist like a dull blade in my chest, and something rises up inside me, an incantation I tried to forget. I part my lips to speak, everything in me ready to boil over, but all at once, the birds stop falling. I look up, my heart gone cold, and the sky is so strange and plain and quiet.

Samuel scoffs. "About time," he says and curses under his breath before retreating into the stable. He'll lose a whole day to sweeping away feathers from inside the fence. One more reason for him to hate me.

I keep moving, glancing back only once at Anna's window, but nobody's there now. If she was ever there at all. I'm probably looking for someone where there's only a shadow.

At the end of the lane, the school doors swing open, and children dash out, chortling on the front lawn, tossing up limp feathers like paper confetti. Their teacher lingers behind them, a thin smile plastered on her terrified face. She glances up at me, and I look away. We used to know each other too. She's another of the girls who would come with us to the forest. Another one who'd rather I disappeared for good now.

Down the road, back at the general store, others start trickling home as well, their ragged boots crunching thousands of hollow bones on the cobblestone road.

It's my turn to go home too. I take the long way out of town along a lonely dirt path that eventually leads up to the main road, and as I pass the last house in the village, Samuel's words echo in my mind.

They're gone for now.

For now. We live perpetually in the present tense. There's no lingering in yesterday, the weight of our grief too heavy to bear. No point in worrying about tomorrow. Between famine and witchfinders, we have no guarantee of any moment past this one. Today is all that counts.

Except that won't be enough to save us. The villagers believe if only they could cup their hands over my mouth and keep me quiet a little longer, this will all turn out fine. They don't understand the logic of witchfinders. How these men are patient, how they'll circle back around eventually. Just because they've moved on for now doesn't mean they've forgotten us.

They've got all the time in the world to murder us.

Right before the crossroads, I hesitate. Something is twitching up ahead in the dirt. A single crow, its wings broken, the beak split down the middle. It's barely alive now. I rush to it and draw it up into my arms, cradling it to my chest, willing it to live. We've lost so many today, but not all of the birds have to leave me. I could keep one. I could save one. That won't make up for the rest, but it will make up for something.

Only it's already too late. The bird goes limp in my arms, and I gag down a sob, resting my forehead against its silent chest, listening for a heartbeat that won't return. Something else I've lost, one more thing I couldn't save.

"Will you please give him to us?" a small voice asks, startling me.

A little girl, no more than six years old, is standing next to me, flashing a gap-toothed grin. There are other children behind her, a whole line of them, faces down, stringy hair slung over their eyes. In front of them, as reverent as an altar, is a wooden wagon packed with dead birds, their bodies crumpled, their slick feathers glinting in the noonday sun.

I inch away. "What are you doing with all of them?"

The little girl curls up her nose. "Burying them of course," she says, as though she could have no other reason. "Will you give him to us now?"

I swallow hard, clutching the crow, the contents of that wagon whirling my stomach. It's a grotesque sight to behold, the stench of death wafting from it like steam off summer stone. Maybe it's not so odd though. Maybe their parents turned them loose to tidy up the streets, commanding them to pluck the broken bodies off the cobblestone and get rid of them. After all, somebody needs to clean up the mess they think I made.

I need to help clean this up as well. With a shaky hand, I pass the crow to the little girl, and she lays him on the top of the pile. She gives me another grin.

"Come with us, Odette," she says, and before I can argue, she's leading the way, the procession drifting forward, her and her friends humming sweetly out of tune.

I follow behind, wanting to know where they're headed. These aren't the same children that were skipping from the school. I've never seen any of them before. Other than the little girl, I haven't seen them even now. Their hair over their eyes, faces turned away, I can't get a good look. They're walking right in front of me, but it's like I'm staring at shadows.

The little girl turns back. "Did the birds do something to make you angry?" she asks, and the question hits me hard, nearly stopping me where I stand.

"No," I whisper.

I loved these birds. The other girls and I would call to them in the forest, drawing them down to us. The crows with their seashells wrapped in twine, the magpies with their shiny nests, the blue jays always with something new to say. After what the witchfinders did, I've waited for years for the birds to come back, never expecting it to be like this. That's because magic is a curious thing. It has a tendency to boil up in unexpected ways. I've tried so hard to keep myself from speaking, from chanting, from howling at the moon. But with all this grief stitched up inside me, everything I want is going wild.

The little girl looks ahead on the road. "We're almost there," she says, and that's when I see it—the sloping hill of the village graveyard. I should have guessed this was our destination. Where else would we go for a funeral?

Inside, past the splintered gate, the rows are cramped and overgrown, half the tombstones crumbling to dust. It's a small plot of land, but there are hundreds of graves, bodies practically stacked atop bodies, dating back for decades, every cause of death you can imagine. Plague and consumption and heartbreak. Too young, too old, too many witches to count. I walk atop the grass, imagining the corpses beneath, remembering how I should be here too.

By now, everyone in the village knows the story. How five years ago, the witchfinders caught me at dawn and dragged me screaming to the town square. How they tied me to a pyre and lit the flame. How I got away anyhow, the only witch in our village ever to escape. Most of my family wasn't so lucky. Aunts and cousins and both my parents, turned to cinders. Only my sister Freya survived, and that's because she took off before the men came for her too.

The children pull the wagon through the center of the cemetery, and I lag behind them, doing my best not to glance at the names on the headstones. By the looks of it, I've already been close enough, small mounds of earth piled here and there. I wish I knew what I did in this place at night, but besides bits and pieces of my memories—the pungent scent of earth, the worms wriggling between my fingers—everything else dissolves in the light of day.

We reach a far corner, and the little girl deposits the crow at my feet. "This one's yours," she says, and with a sharp laugh, she skips several rows over to inter three pale sparrows next to a disintegrating mausoleum.

All around me, the other children dig tiny graves too, their fingernails limned with soil, the same as mine. I try to watch them, but they move too quickly, so I still never get a look at their faces. I can't even count how many there are. Seven, I think, or maybe ten, or it could be more than that. Hell, they might even outnumber the villagers. Giggling to one another, they snatch the dead birds from the wagon and abandon them one by one in the ground. A cardinal, a kingfisher, a sparrow. The steady thud of small, mangled bodies, tumbling into the earth, followed by a gentle shuffle of dirt to hide them, feathers and all, in the dark.

The sound sets my skin buzzing, and I drop the bag of salt next to me and kneel, wanting to get this over with. The ground is soft in my hands. It should be frozen, but this earth is so restless, always being dug up, either by the gravediggers or by me.

"This will be over soon," I whisper to the crow, but when I pick him up, he twitches again. Just for an instant, one wink of that glossy eye as though he's looking straight at me.

"He's not dead," I say, glancing up, and they're suddenly everywhere. The other children circling me. Though their faces still aren't clear, I can see their eyes now, faded to a charmless gray. One after another, they move closer, and something in me tells me to scream, but all I can do is stare at them as I hold the crow tighter.

The little girl pushes to the front, forcing the rest back a step. "Not yet," she says to them, snapping her tongue. "Don't spoil the game."

The other children retreat, slipping behind tombstones, hair falling in their faces again, their eyes vanishing altogether. Beside me, the little girl finishes loosening the ground with both hands and gingerly places the crow inside.

"There," she says, and that's the last one. All the birds they gathered are nestled beneath us. The rest of the children tow the now-empty wagon toward the cemetery gate, everything about them blurry like smears of fresh paint.

I pick up the salt, my fingers aching in the cold, and look to the little girl. "What game? What are all of you playing?"

She gazes up at me, grinning again. "Why don't you come with us? That way, we can show you."

My mouth dry, I only shake my head.

She shrugs. "Your loss," she says and follows the others along the winding path. Back to collect more birds from the streets, I suspect, but I don't stay to find out.

Instead, I'm running now. Out of the cemetery, down past the crossroads, and up into the forest that always remembers my name. It's two miles through rocky terrain, but I make a journey that took me more than an hour this morning in only a few minutes. Anything to get away from that village.

My cottage materializes between the trees, and I waste no time. My hands quivering, I circle the four oak walls, no more than a shack, pouring a thick line of salt around the perimeter. I make sure not to miss one spot, not even a space so small as the width of my thumb. So long as I do it right, this will seal out the darkness. This will keep me safe, at least for a little while.

When I'm finished, the cottage is already unlocked and waiting for me. Inside, everything is as I left it. A cold hearth, a cold bed. There's one window in the corner and a splintered cupboard that's nearly empty. This home is a shell, the sagging walls echoing only my footsteps back to me. I've lived here ever since I fled the village. Other witches were the caretakers before me, women who knew exile intimately. Women who are long gone now, bestowing this place to whoever found it. Across the room, everything they left behind is locked away in a dusty hope chest. Stones and dried herbs and a litany of spells scribbled on crumbling papyrus more delicate than a moth's wings. There are spell bottles too, filled with nails and pins and sprigs of rosemary that never wilt, all these dreams left undone. If you listen, you can almost hear them whispering, these witches the world forgot.

There's another whisper as well, carrying on the wind from miles away, this one not from a witch but from a man who hopes to silence every woman like me.

Come to me, Odette. That voice, rich and cruel and terrifyingly familiar. I close my eyes and see him there in the capital with his black boots and black heart.

The voices in a witch's head are infinite. You speak to the earth, the sky, the distant, the dead. Sometimes, you wish you could recognize who's murmuring in your ear. Other times, all you want is to forget their name.

"Leave me alone," I say, desperate to escape, desperate to be free of him. I clench my teeth, and something flickers inside me. The birds. I feel them, twitching in the dirt, their tousled bodies a kaleidoscope of feathers, their beaks gnashing at the darkness. I'm not trying to call to them, but that doesn't matter because they hear me now, and they want to help. When I open my eyes, the crows and cardinals and goldfinches aren't in the cemetery anymore. None of the birds are. They're right outside in my garden, digging their way up through the earth.

And they're coming straight for me.

chapter two

THE BIRDS ARE EVERYWHERE AT ONCE, SLIDING UP OUT OF THE DIRT AND surrounding my cottage, their beaks sharper than I remember, their eyes the color of an unforgiving midnight. I hold my breath as their weightless feet scurry across the moss on the thatched roof, their silken feathers whispering against the other side of the window.

Then the air sparks around me, and they're not outside anymore. They slip through the walls, the mortar, the cracks in the grout. They come down the chimney, push under the doors.

"Please," I say, but nothing will stop them now. High among the rafters, they circle me, and then they descend together—toward me and into me. I cover my face with both hands as all the birds glide right through my body, their wings tickling the inside of my rib cage.

They're here and not here, mere specters of what they once were. They make no sound, their beautiful melodies silent in their throats. Death must have stolen their voices, the same way it steals everything else.

"I'm sorry," I whisper, and with my eyes closed, I reach out toward them, palms turned upward. I won't fight this. They can take me with them for all I care. They can carry me off into the darkness.

Except it's too late for that. Already, they're starting to fade. They're not as strong as they once were, not as strong as when I called to them in the forest all those full moons ago. Another thrash of their wings, and the room goes quiet.

I open my eyes again and move toward the window, steadying myself against the sill. Outside, the day has forgotten them. No doves burrowing through the dirt, no cardinals streaking through the sky like blood. It's as though the birds never existed at all. And maybe they didn't. Maybe I'm imagining all of this. A frail mind at the end of a long day, envisioning ghosts where there's only emptiness.

I shiver and draw my jacket tighter around me. My fingertips have gone numb, my whole body is nearly numb, and I need to ignite the fire. I need to keep myself alive. But when I turn around, something else is waiting there for me.

A crow curled before the hearth, his wings broken, his beak split. This is the same bird I found at the crossroads, the one I was desperate to save, the one the little girl buried.

Perhaps I'm not imagining ghosts after all.

I inch closer to the crow, scooping him up with both hands. Even now, he's so terribly beautiful, his wingspan almost wider than my outstretched arms, the divots on his dark feathers soft and smooth. He never moves, not a blink, not a breath, but I know it doesn't have to be that way. There are strange things a witch can do, even if she shouldn't. I could coax him back to me. I could cast every spell I know to keep him here. Anything so this cottage might not be so lonely anymore.

Then I shake my head and remember. This is no longer a house of magic. That's the rule I made for myself, and it's one I shouldn't break. My hands trembling, I button my coat up to the collar and carry him out to the garden. Ice hangs in the air, glinting like shards of broken diamonds. Though I don't want to let him go, I know this is the right way. I tuck him against the frozen earth, and he nestles there between rows of lavender, wilted in the winter frost, his eyes filmed over, his chest silent and still.

"Go," I whisper to him. "Be free."

These words should be enough. If he can rise from the grave, then he can rise from here. And that's exactly what he does because when I trudge back into my cottage, there he is, curled up by the hearth as lifeless as before.

"You have to stop," I say and take him out to the other side of the property, a little farther into the forest, a little farther away from me.

He's back by lunchtime, waiting inside my cabinet behind the dried spices. I rasp out a small scream when I find him there, those slick black feathers clogging up a pot of crystallized honeycomb.

"This is ridiculous," I say, cradling him in my arms, scowling at him like he's a wayward child. "Go on now. I can't help you."

There's no reason for him to keep returning. I'm a witch with nothing to offer. No warmth in my home, no magic at my hearth. He'd be better off anywhere but here.

And that's where I'll take him—far enough into the forest that he won't want to return. My coat pulled around me tighter than before, I place him inside a basket I use for gathering herbs, folding an old handkerchief around him like a shroud. It will keep him warm until we get to where we're going.

With the afternoon whispering ice and lies on the wind, I slip between elms and birches, the basket clasped tight against me. Overhead, the branches are all stripped bare, the pale bark like sun-bleached bone, and a drizzle of rain drips down tree trunks, clinging to the stiff grass, the remnants of a winter that hasn't quite thawed yet, hasn't quite let us go. A month or two from now, living will be a bit easier, but today, it's still February, and February is nothing if not cruel.

My body heaves with the chill, and I look for a place to leave the crow, somewhere familiar for him. It's been so long though, and there's no tangle of nests left in the trees, no sign that the birds were ever here. Perhaps he's like me now. Perhaps he doesn't belong anywhere either.

I wish I could keep him with me, perched on my shoulder, safe in my arms, but that's not how magic works. If I conjure him back to me like this, he'll only be a marionette, his hollow bones twitching and restless but his heart muted in his chest. I can make him move, make him pretend to be alive, maybe even do a passable job of it. But a witch can't reverse death, no matter how much she wishes she could. If he's a ghost, let him be a ghost but don't make him become something worse.

What's left of him will be happier in the woods. That's what I keep telling myself.

The path becomes rockier, everything in the world closing in around me, and all at once, I'm not alone. Something familiar echoes between the trees. It's such a tiny sound, so fragile, so distant, but I recognize it. It's the lonely call of the birds.

A pang of hope prickles in my chest. Maybe these ones are different, alive and rising from the trees, not collapsing from the sky. Maybe the birds are returning to us like I'd always hoped. I move toward the sound of their voices, but the breeze changes and carries them away from me.

"Wait," I say, their melody dissipating like smoke, and I stagger forward, searching every crevice in the earth as if they might be hiding there. I'm not watching the path before me, never noticing when it narrows or becomes overgrown or disappears altogether.

Something else disappears too. It's not just the birds who have gone silent. Deeper into the woods, there's no chirping of insects, no rustling of leaves. Everything is quiet now, and I remember what Beatrix used to tell my sister Freya and me when we were young—how the worst sound in the forest is no sound at all.

My guts grind together, and I try to turn back, but the trees mirror themselves on all sides, imprisoning me in their own reflection.

A trick. The forest tricked me. After all these years, I should have known better. But then it shouldn't be so easy to stumble into the Hyland Forest.

The sun is brighter now, and my coat clings heavy to my body, sweat already beading on my upper lip. Even though everywhere else is barren this time of year, the trees are always verdant in the Hyland Forest, the flowers blossoming in bright scarlets and violets and midnight blues, clusters of boneset flowers as pale as fresh cream.

I edge forward, shielding my eyes. All of this was ours once. I used to bring Anna and the other girls here, our long hair hanging down in tendrils, our laughter ricocheting off the sky. Hands entwined, we'd cast a circle and call out to the birds, exhaling a long whistle, sweet and sharp. They'd always come to us, perching all around, chattering their own spells to the sky. We used to be safe here, but now with no more birds and no more girls, this land is haunted and hungry for magic left undone.

And that's what the Hyland Forest wants from me. It craves a witch to finish what we started, and now here I am, having accidentally wandered into its embrace. My head hums softly, and I close my eyes, reminders of the past everywhere around me, interred in the earth, whispered on the wind. Spells without mouths to speak them, love charms for hearts that no longer beat, bottles buried in the dirt over grudges that hardly matter now. I should run, but my body sinks into the earth, inch by inch, the mud slick between my toes, and something in this place tells me I should stay a little longer.

Next to me, my shoes are kicked off. I don't remember doing that, but with the wind murmuring my name, I don't really care either.

This is another trick, someone says, maybe someone with my voice, maybe even me, but I pretend not to listen. It's warm, and the air is fragrant with honeysuckle and mugwort, everything earthy and inviting. For the first time in years, I want to remember. All this magic, all these memories. The spells start flooding back into me, and I open my mouth to speak, but what comes out doesn't belong to me. Instead, my throat contracts, and a thousand voices fill me up, buzzing in my bones like common horseflies.

Stay with us.

Please stay this time, Odette.

Don't ever leave again.

I don't recognize these voices. They're coming from elsewhere, ghosts I've never met. Ghosts that are more than ready to meet me.

My blood simmers in my veins, and I feel my legs sinking deeper into the earth as though I'm becoming the knotted roots of an ancient tree. Something that belongs here, that never gets to leave.

My body goes slack, the basket slipping from my hands and into the grass. The crow. He's still inside. I reach for him, stretching and contorting my arms through the mud, but the Hyland Forest is too quick for me. It shudders once before the ground opens up, and I cry out, helpless, as the crow is swallowed up by the earth, the same way I'm being swallowed up.

This can't be how I end too. The forest is still singing its honeyed lies to me, but I brace against the grass and lift myself up. The shadows are longer now, more ravenous than before. I yank my boots out of the dirt and push past the flowers turning their blooms to watch me as though I'm the sun and they're eager to drink me in.

I surge toward the trees, but they push me back again, the branches twisting me around until I don't know which direction is which. There has to be a way out. It's a rule my mother taught me: so long as there's a breath left in you, you can always break a spell.

Briars biting at my skin, I keep going until I reach a cluster of willows where the air gets murky and strange. This must be the edge of the forest where I came in. I step forward, staring into this enchantment that mirrors all the trees back to me. It's like a looking glass, which means it can break like one too.

My hand draws back, and with a sharp breath, I bring my fist down on the thick air. At once, the reflection of the forest fragments all around me, and I tumble through the trees and back out into the light, the chill of winter enveloping me.

My head whirls, and I'm standing now on the road that leads to the village. This isn't where I'd hoped to be, but that doesn't matter. When you leave the

Hyland Forest, you never know where you'll come out.

And more than that, you never know who will be there on the other side. This is the final trick the woods have played on me today, dropping me here where I'm not alone. My heart in my throat, I turn around and see someone on the dirt road. It's a man who doesn't belong here, a face I've never seen before. My body seizes up, and all I can think is it's one of them. It's a witchfinder come back to set the countryside alight.

A hundred paces away, he's so close now, which means it's too late for me to run without being seen. I grit my teeth, an incantation blossoming in my throat. Already, I envision cursing him, of speaking the words I used to teach the other girls, a mere phrase or two that could send him wandering into a day that won't ever end. After all, there's always a fairy ring somewhere nearby, willing to gobble down a bemused traveler.

As he draws nearer, he spots me at the side of the road, and though I make no effort to greet him, he waves brightly anyway.

"Hello there," he says, heading toward me, and my lips part, ready to direct him into a sweet oblivion.

But my chest constricts, and I remember the promise I made to myself. No magic, especially not dark magic, especially not against a stranger. For all I know, he's as lost and hopeless as I am. I can't assume every man is a witchfinder, can I?

The incantation retreats within me, and I stand a little taller, pretending I'm not afraid. "May I help you?" I say, the words weak and inadequate compared to what I could have spoken.

He grins, dimples marking his cheeks. "Could you please tell me which way to the nearest village?"

That would be *our* village. He wants to go to the place where I grew up, but I don't know if I want him there. It's not my home, not anymore, but somehow, it doesn't feel right to send this stranger to them. If anyone is going to bother my village, it should be me, not a man who could be anyone at all.

His grin never fading, he inches toward me, closing the gulf between us, and my body rises up, nearly quivering off the ground, still desperate to escape. I strain through the whispering sound of the wind to hear other voices in these parts, but it's just the two of us now, the crow and the other birds lost to me. I could dart back into the woods, vanishing between the birch trees and hemlock lace, but this man will then know I have a reason to run. And he'll have a reason to pursue. So I steady myself instead, inspecting him up and down.

Worn brown leather boots, small satchel, thin coat. No horse in sight and no bible to beat.

From the looks of it, he's common enough, as plain as all the rest of us. This is a good sign. The witchfinders are fancier. They arrive with flair, armed with pomp and circumstance and enough iron and flint to ignite a whole village. In the past, they've always appeared on our streets, clumped together in cliques of threes and fours, their black boots and black cloaks designed to put you on edge as though they're already mourning you before you've even died.

This man is nothing like them. Here he is, coming not from the north, from the city that makes witchfinders the same way it makes sharp mead and wagon wheels, but from farther to the east, the direction of the other villages where everyone is just as afraid as we are.

"Well?" he asks, flashing me that smile as warm as summer rot. "Can you help me?"

I back away a few steps, my stomach churning. Even if he isn't a witchfinder, that still doesn't make him a friend. This is a cruel tale as old as time. Terrible things often start with a girl meeting a strange man in the forest. And after everything that's happened, I won't fall prey to another terrible thing.

My hands curl into claws, and an incantation rises inside me again. "What exactly do you need in the village?"

"To visit family," he says. "I'm Samuel Fontaine's nephew."

Instantly, the ground goes cold beneath me, and I unclench my hands. He's Anna's cousin. That changes everything. If I send him astray, the villagers will be more vexed than usual with me. Harm their kin, and I won't have to wait for the witchfinders to build a pyre. My former friends would be more than happy to bring the fire to me.

I motion toward the crossroads. "Head that way," I say. "Stay on this path, and you won't miss it, not even if you try."

And believe me, I want to say, *I've tried for years to escape that village.*

The man smiles again. "Thank you," he says, but he doesn't move from this spot, doesn't go on his way like he should, doesn't do anything except stare into me as though he already owns me. "May I be of any help to you now, madam?"

I withdraw from him just a little, just enough to open the gap between us.

This isn't right. I've done what he's asked. I've answered his question. Why can't that be enough?

"Like I said"—I motion again with a flick of my hand—"it's that way to the crossroads."

Please leave, I keep thinking. *Be on your way and quit bothering me.*

Why is it so impossible for people to leave witches alone? You'd think we'd naturally scare them off. Instead, they're drawn to us, even when they don't know what we are, even when we look like ordinary girls to them, so-called helpless maidens in need of their saving.

Except today is different. He's the one in need of help, a lost traveler like all the rest. It's so easy to go missing. There's a zigzag of roads in this part of the countryside, and it's not as though you can simply shortcut through the forest. Travelers always make up excuses to themselves about why they can't set foot among these trees—too tired, too cold, no compass, no time—but even as they walk the well-worn road, their eyes constantly dart up to the canopy, silently testing the perimeter with their gazes, wondering why some land simply doesn't welcome them. Men like him must be particularly displeased since they feel that everything belongs to them the moment they see it.

He must see something else he thinks should be his because he motions behind me. "Is that yours?"

I look back toward the forest. The children's wagon is hidden there at the edge of the trees.

"Yes, that's mine," I blurt out, though I don't know why. It's no crime for the little girl and her friends to be out, singing their strange songs, burying their dead birds. Yet this man shouldn't be privy to any of that. He doesn't seem like the kind who will understand a place like this.

"You better not forget it when you go," he says, and at last, he starts toward the village. "I'll tell Anna and Samuel you send your regards."

On the road, his figure folds in on itself, becoming smaller and smaller until he vanishes like fog. I watch him go, thinking how he never asked me who I was, so he can't possibly send them my respects. All the better. They don't want to hear from me anyway.

I'm ready to be on my way too when a shadow moves at the corner of my eye.

"Has he finally gone?" That tiny voice like untrimmed fingernails scratching against metal. It's the little girl, emerging as if from nowhere.

"Where did you come from?" I ask, my voice thin.

She mashes a piece of frozen grass between her fingers. "I was right here the whole time."

Right here. In a place where there are no tall weeds, no ravine, no ditches to conceal her. She should have been easy to spot. She should have had nowhere to hide. It's not as though she could go into the forest, not without a witch's steady hand to guide her there.

I hesitate, a lump twisting in the back of my throat. "What are you doing out alone?"

She hunches down, scrounging through the dirt, her fingers stained with earth. "Looking for decorations for the birds' graves," she says. "Do you know where I can find the flowers, Odette?"

Dread coils through me, part of me convinced she already knows about me. About where I've been and what I've seen today.

"I'm sorry," I say, "but it's winter. There aren't any flowers left."

The little girl gazes up at me. "Are you sure about that?"

Still kneeling in the dirt, she keeps watching me, keeps waiting for me to answer, her eyes darker than before, but I shake my head. She's only a child, nothing more. This day, this forest, has spooked me. It's trying to convince me of things that can't possibly be true.

"You need to go home," I say and turn away, ready to take my own advice, but when I start to move, something metallic crunches beneath my boot.

I jump back and see it there in the dirt. A necklace. That man must have dropped it. My fingers trembling, I pick it up and turn it over in my hand, flicking open the locket to reveal a hand-drawn portrait inside. A young woman stares back at me, a dimple in her chin, a valance of red hair across her eyes.

"Who is she?" The little girl is suddenly next to me, her steps on the frozen earth never making a sound.

"I'm not sure," I say and hold the necklace up to the light, the thick chain shimmering in the remains of the afternoon. It's made of pure silver, probably worth more than I am.

With only one coin left to my name, I think how I could keep this. I could tuck it in my pocket and use it to bargain my way through this winter and the next. A satchel of flour, a barrel of salt, enough lard to feed a small army. This simple talisman, so disposable to him that he lost it on a whim, could make the next year bearable for me.

Then something in the picture flickers, a flash of light behind the eyes, as if the image is alive if only for a moment. Shame rises up inside me, my resolve withering at once. This isn't mine. It's an heirloom, and I shouldn't keep it. At least that way, no one can call me a thief.

"Come on," I say to the little girl as I head toward the village to return the necklace. The stranger will make it there before us, no doubt, but if we're quick enough, we shouldn't be too far behind him.

Overhead, the sun is sinking in the sky, and I shiver in the cold. The little girl plods a few steps behind me, pulling the wagon through thick mud. I wish she'd hurry. I don't like staying out after dark. There are strange things that come looking for a witch in the night.

"Do you need help?" I ask, holding out my hand to take the wagon from her.

She recoils. "No," she says, her nose scrunched up, her face pink with chill. "Nobody touches this but us."

I exhale a weary laugh, my breath fogging around me. "I was only trying to help," I say, even though I should know by now that nobody from that village ever wants my help.

Together, she and I reach the crossroads with four directions to go, the same as this morning, the same as always. The little girl understands this. Her gaze goes dark again, and she watches the horizon as though expecting something to materialize there.

"Let's not go back to the village," she says.

I gape at her. "Why not?"

"Because," she says as though that's enough of an answer. "I don't like it there. I don't like those people. Let's go somewhere else."

"How about your friends?" I ask. "Don't you like them?"

"Not enough to go back," she says, watching me now, her eyes wide and unblinking. "Can't you do a spell or something? To get us away from here?"

My cheeks burn, and regret settles through me. "Not anymore," I say. "I don't do that now."

I turn to the west to start toward the village, but the little girl won't move, her face pinched, her feet fixed in the dirt.

"What kind of witch are you?" She glares at me, one hand on the wagon, the other curled into a tiny fist. "Must not be a very good one. Maybe that's why the witchfinders let you live."

I seize up in the middle of the crossroads, rage lurching through me. "Nobody *let* me live," I say.

This must be what the villagers claim—not that I nearly died, not that I escaped, but that I just wasn't worth killing in the first place.

Jaw clenched, I want to scream. I want to tell her that what she heard about me is all wrong, but there's no point. She won't listen anyhow. They never do. The best I can manage is to keep walking and leave her behind me. This little girl found her way out of the village, so she can find her own way back. She's not my responsibility. These days, nobody is.

Only I don't get away from her that easily. With guilt blossoming crimson across her face, she catches up and walks right next to me, closer than before, the wagon tottering behind her.

"I'm sorry," she whispers, but I pretend not to hear her. I pretend she's not here at all, and part of me wonders if I might be right. There are so many haunted things in this countryside. Maybe she's just another one.

When we finally cross into the village, the sun is almost gone, the dull yellow of the parting day spilling out across the horizon like the broken yolk of an egg. My feet are blistered. I've made this trip twice today, two times too many, and this is it, the last reason I've got for coming back. This village can live without me. I want to live without this village too.

In the town square among the charred cobblestones, there are people congregating. At first, I assume they're here to gather up the birds, but all those bodies—the ones the children didn't already bury in the graveyard—have been shoved aside, the loose feathers piled up in grimy alleys. Something else has got the villagers transfixed, something right there near the place where the burn marks never faded. At the back of the crowd, among the dull murmurs of restless spectators, I hesitate, blending in with the rest, trying to catch a glimpse of what they're doing.

"What is it?" the little girl says, but I shake my head. The local men stand in front, always in front, blocking the way. They're working on something, the piercing melody of their hammers setting my teeth on edge, but from here, it's impossible to see what they're doing, and I don't want to stay to find out. I already know I'm not welcome, so before anyone spots me, I maneuver through the crowd, my head down, the noise of the square fading into a dull buzz behind me. Crisscrossing through alleys, I kick up tufts of pale down that lilt in the air like fresh pollen, always careful to avoid the street where I used to live.

At last, I reach the threshold of Anna and Samuel's house, and with an unsteady hand, I knock on the door, my mind still humming with what I've seen in the square. It's so familiar, so achingly familiar. That sound. The pounding of heavy nails against splintered wood, the kind that isn't meant to last. It's meant to burn.

Even though I don't want it to, the truth catches in my throat, choking me like a crust of week-old bread. They're building a pyre. The villagers are building a pyre, which can only mean one thing.

The witchfinders are returning.

I exhale a ragged breath, ready to cry out just as the lock turns on the other side, and Samuel appears, as gray as a phantom in the doorway. He stares out at me, his eyes colorless and defeated, seeing all and nothing at the same time. Behind him, Anna is hunched over the hearth, her dark hair in her face as if she's been weeping. And though no one will look at him, the man from the road sits proudly at the head of the table. The door creaks open wider, and he glances up, his face beaming when he sees that it's me.

"Here's the young lady I was telling you about," he says, "the one who showed me the way here."

Anna looks to me now, her cheeks flushed, her brow twisted. "Odette?" She speaks my name like it's a curse. "You did this?"

"A wonderfully helpful girl." The man smiles, his pale teeth glinting in the glow of the fire. "Everyone in the capital will be happy to hear how much more agreeable this village has become."

His words spin my head. The capital. He's from the capital. He's one of them.

I've led a witchfinder right to us.

chapter three

I WAVER AT THE THRESHOLD, TRYING TO SPEAK OR SCREAM, BUT ALL THAT comes out is a strangled wheeze.

"I didn't know who you were," I say finally, not for his benefit but so the rest of the family knows. "You only told me you were Anna and Samuel's kin."

The man exhales a braying laugh. "I appreciate the help regardless," he says and motions me to the table. "Come now. Have supper with us."

A meal. With him. As though I could break bread with a monster.

"I'm not hungry," I say, and for a moment, his eyes flash dark, and everything in the room goes still, Anna's hand frozen on the wooden spoon suspended over the pot in the fire, Samuel's face contorted as if in pain.

Without a word, we all know that I've broken an unspoken rule: no one is permitted to deny a witchfinder. We learned this lesson the hard way the last time they were here.

My body starts to drift backward, away from this man, away from this place, but he keeps staring into me, his unrepentant gaze the color of brackish water. I wonder if he might pry open my jaw and spoon gruel and stringy beef down my throat just to make me eat this dinner, just to prove a point.

But that's not what he does at all. He simply smiles again.

"Even if you aren't hungry," he says and rises from his chair, "you could still come in and sit a while."

My breath whirls in my chest, and he starts toward me, his back hunched slightly, like a wild animal eager to pounce.

Behind me, the alley is empty. The little girl must have gotten wise and finally gone home. I envy her for that.

"Come," the man says again, and Samuel falls back a step to make way for him. "Stay with us."

The witchfinder doesn't understand I'm not welcome. I could take a seat at the table, but that isn't what Samuel wants. It isn't what Anna wants either. She watches me from the hearth, her accusing gaze asking me the same question over and over. *How could you lead him here?*

Another step, and the man is standing right in front of me. He's going to reach out for me. This witchfinder, this gentleman maniac, is going to touch me. I should run, faster than the north wind, faster than any fire could sear my flesh, but it won't do me any good. Because if I flee, he'll know I have something to hide.

My lips part, but I can't speak. All my words are failing me now. The spells I memorized long ago wither on my tongue. For years, I've told myself to forget. Maybe I did too good a job.

I lean against the doorframe, my head heavy, and something jingles in my pocket. It's the necklace this man lost on the road, the reason I came back to the village. I press my hand across the pocket to silence it, and that's when I hear her.

Tell him tomorrow, a voice whispers, a voice I've never heard before. This is the face inside the locket, the girl he left behind. Her words thrum right into my blood. *Tell him you'll come back tomorrow.*

The pot on the hearth boils over, and I sway backward, a step closer to freedom.

"How about tomorrow?" I say, everything in me held tight.

He stares into me, his hands trembling as if he's about to reach out and take hold of me. "You'll have supper with us then?"

I nod, swallowing a heavy mouthful of air.

"All right," he says, and with a stiff smile, I curtsy at him like a proper young lady and vanish into the street before he has a chance to stop me.

The houses smear past me as I shortcut around the square and the hideous sight of those pyres. I slip between buildings, crossing through backyards where I'm not invited, careful that I'm not spotted, trespassing in broad daylight.

I finally step out onto a familiar street, standing somewhere I never wanted to see again.

The burned-out shell of my childhood home.

There's practically nothing left, only the outline of a foundation and the debris of a life that no one's bothered to scrub away. The villagers are too superstitious to pillage the ash for valuables. My family was worth little when they were alive and even less now that they're dead.

A sharp wind, bitter enough to make your teeth ache, cuts through the air, and I shudder. I don't like to come here, but she won't be long. She never is.

I breathe in, and next to me, she appears like an apparition with those same ruddy cheeks and hair as dark as a witch's cauldron. Anna. I know how she got here—sneaking out her bedroom window, creeping between the houses, the same way she used to do when we were girls. And she knew I'd be here in the street in front of my house, waiting for her like I always did before.

I can barely look at her, shame settling in my belly. "I'm so sorry," I say, folding and unfolding my hands in front of me. "I had no idea who he was. He told me he was your family."

"That's just it," she whispers. "He *is* family. A cousin we haven't seen in years."

She and I stand side by side, the first time we've been alone together in years. It's been so long yet no time at all. Up close, Anna looks the same with her bright and curious eyes. I suppose I don't look so different either. It's strange how time can decimate you on the inside but not change you much on the outside. A face should bear a mark for this much loss, some kind of signpost saying, *This is real. This happened.* But the cruelest trick of all is how quickly the world forgets.

The shrill melody from the square carries through the streets, the hammering of nails sizzling in my blood.

"Why did he come alone?" I ask. "The witchfinders have never done that before."

She shakes her head. "That's because he isn't one of them, not yet," she says. "He's here to prove himself. To get in their good graces."

A witchfinder in training. That pyre in the square, made for nobody and everybody. He doesn't care who he burns so long as it's enough to impress the other men in the capital.

"You aren't safe under the same roof as him," I whisper.

She shrugs. "It's my home," she says. "Where else can I go?"

We look at each other, both of us already knowing that answer.

I turn away and gaze at what's left of the house. Not much now. Blackened wood in makeshift piles, a splintered table leg, a pale shard that could be dust-caked porcelain or could be a bit of bone. I don't want to know which it is.

There's something else too, glinting in the afternoon sun, tucked beneath the ash in a far corner of the foundation.

"What do you see?" Anna asks, but I shake my head.

"It's nothing," I say, but even from here, I know exactly what it is. A small bottle of port wine, one that's almost forty years old. It's from my parents' wedding, saved for a special occasion that never came. Now it sours in the sun, forgotten in plain sight. I won't cross the threshold for it. I've never set foot in this house again, not since the night it was turned to cinders. Nothing feels like mine anymore.

"Anna?" Samuel's voice echoes through the streets. "Where are you?"

My chest constricts. *Don't,* I want to say to her. *Don't go back there.*

Anna's cheeks flush as though she can hear me. "I have to," she says, and before I can argue, she vanishes between the other cottages, leaving me alone with my ghosts.

I never should have stayed, not in this village, not in this forest. I should have left years ago. My sister Freya was smarter than I was. She ran the first chance she got. She knew how this would go. That while the witchfinders are more than happy to murder anyone, it's easy to guess who they'll choose first: a mother, a sister, a daughter. Something about a woman's burning body enlivens these men. How much sweeter our melting flesh must smell to them, like clumps of sugar crystallizing in a kettle.

The sun is almost gone, and the villagers are starting to filter home. Something stirs inside me, my mind going dizzy, and I need to get back too. I shuffle through the streets, past Beatrix's seamstress shop and the tavern where Freya and I retrieved our father too many times to count. He was more of a ghost to us than all the bones in the graveyard put together. Thanks to our father, Freya and I learned how you could hold someone's hand as tight as you could and still never reach them.

I keep going, hoping no one notices me, but at the very next corner, I nearly collide with the blacksmith and his family. His wife gapes at me, and we recognize each other at once. She's another of the girls who used to venture into the woods, dancing and chanting and calling out to the sky. Now here she is, her face lined and scared, ushering her family home before dark.

"Why is everyone helping him?" Her daughter looks up at her. "Why don't we do something?"

"Hush now," her mother says, nudging her on, and I swallow a sob because I wish we could explain all of this. How the villagers never want to, how they don't have a choice. If you even try to say no, someone else will construct the pyre and then you'll be the first to burn.

The witchfinders never lift a finger of course. They won't get their hands dirty because they don't have to. That's almost the worst part—how they make us build our own graves.

I'm nearly to the crossroads when my head starts to spin again, faster this time, the dark shapes at the edge of my vision pressing closer to me.

"Not now," I whisper, my guts turning liquid, my vision blurring. I'm desperate to get to the forest, but even as I break into a sprint, it's already too late. All my muscles go soft and useless, and the whole world fades to gray as I'm torn away from myself.

When I open my eyes, I'm kneeling in the cemetery, my arms plunged elbow-deep into the earth.

The sky is black, night settled like tar on the village, and I wrench myself out of the dirt, toppling backward into the grass. I have no idea how long I've been here. Hours maybe, my hands tangled around bone. A wail blooming in my chest, I want to scream, but I'm not alone. Nearby, something giggles.

"Hello?" My voice is vellum-thin, and I hesitate, not even taking a breath. There's no answer in the shadows, and I won't wait to find out who it is.

My head still hazy, I struggle to my feet and start toward the cemetery gates, not moving too fast, not looking afraid. All around, there's a squeal of wagon wheels and the weight of a dozen eyes on me. I stumble down the dirt path, headed the wrong way, headed toward the village, but with the whispers right behind me, I won't look back.

The horses whinny as I pass the stable, and I hush them, not wanting to wake Samuel. Slipping between houses, staying out of sight, I keep moving, trying to cut through this town and get back to the forest. The voices from the cemetery have faded now, the quiet giggles no longer barbs in my back. Those children, strange and curious and everywhere at once. The little girl must have returned to them when she left me at Anna and Samuel's house earlier. I only wish I knew how I ended up there in the graveyard with them.

With the village dozing all around me, I emerge from a dusty alley, dodging around a mound of stained feathers. I'm on my old street now, and there's someone in front of my house. I move closer, and the moonlight shifts, revealing a world-worn face.

Beatrix. She's gripping a bundle of rosemary and lavender tied with ivory lace, faded as a secondhand wedding dress. I stand next to her on the cobblestone, still several steps back from the house, a safe distance from the past.

"I always try to make an offering to your family at midnight," she says without looking at me. "It's the least I can do."

"It's not your fault what happened," I say.

She turns toward me, her eyes soft and sad. "It's not yours either."

I nod, not quite believing that. A question burns in my chest, one I don't want to ask.

"Do you think the witchfinder is here because of me?" I whisper. "Because of the birds?"

Beatrix hesitates. "I don't know," she says, and I hate myself a little more. Samuel was right. I did bring the witchfinders back to the village after all.

Beatrix places the herbs next to the remains of the house, and something glints in the dirt nearby at the same spot where the front door once was.

"I believe that's yours," she says. My body nearly numb in the midnight chill, I inch closer, one stifled step at a time, until I'm right at the threshold of a house that used to be mine. Another glint of the glass—and I recognize it. The port wine from my parents' wedding. After I left today, Anna must have come back and fished it out of the ash for me.

I pick it up and turn it over in my hand. It's a thin bottle, all dust-caked now, the cork chipped and the wax seal melted away. There can't be much more than two glasses of wine inside. Even the gifts at my parents' wedding weren't extravagant. Our family never had much, but none of the families in this village ever did.

I shove the wine bottle in my jacket pocket. I already have the perfect place for it. Inside the dusty hope chest, it will join the whispering bottles in my cottage, all those spells from the witches who came before, the ones who mended hearts even if it broke their own. The ones who made all the sacrifices and were forgotten for their trouble.

Only I haven't forgotten. As I do my best to remember them, something tightens deep in my bones, and I know what I should do. I should follow in the footsteps of those other witches. Quivering in my pocket, this bottle could be another spell. Something to keep that would-be witchfinder from setting even one more fire in this village.

I could do this, just one more bit of magic, just enough to make things right again. Though I promised myself I'd stopped forever, it wouldn't be so hard to make this small exception.

Beatrix watches me, sensing it in me, the darkness dancing across my face. "What do you need?" she asks, and I smile.

At her shop, I take it from the counter. A box of pins. That's all. So painfully simple, but not every spell has to be complicated.

"What do I owe you?" I ask. "I need to give you something in return for this."

"You already are, Odette," Beatrix says. "If it works, you're giving all of us something."

I want to reach out for her, embrace her, thank her for everything she's done. Ever since my sister and I were children, Beatrix has always been there with a wise word or an ointment for a skinned knee or a place for us to hide when our mother's temper flared at another failed spell. Even now, if I asked, Beatrix would clear a space next to her treadle where we could conjure this spell together. But I wouldn't expect that of her. I need to do this alone. That's the only safe way.

"Thank you," I say and step back out on the darkened street, my body heavier than before.

Down past the crossroads and up into the forest, I never stop, never look back, the frozen grass crunching beneath my boots like brittle bones. The things in the shadows are whipping closer to me now, but I'm almost there. My cottage waits for me in the dark, drowsing in a clearing, surrounded by thin stalks of dead herbs that didn't quite bloom before winter came and silenced them forever.

Inside, I light a fire and sit cross-legged on the bare floor, lining up everything for the spell.

The bottle of wine. A box of pins. The lost necklace on a silver chain. This is all there is and all I need.

In the corner, the other bottles whisper, but I don't open up the hope chest and look at them. I never touch those bottles. They belong to the lost witches, and that isn't my magic to meddle with.

For now, I've got my own spell to conjure. I reach out, ready to begin, but my hands shake, and I recoil. Part of me doesn't want to do this. I promised myself that I'd move on, that I'd let go of magic. But the witchfinders haven't let go of us. I need to do something to stop them even if I don't trust myself. Even if I'm afraid I'll only make this so much worse.

Still trembling, I grasp the bottle and pry the cork free. The heady scent of wine fills the room. I close my eyes and focus, drifting away, nearly rising out of my body, as I grip the necklace. The girl from the locket materializes in my mind, everything about her becoming clearer. A cleft in her chin, tears in her eyes, the family bible clutched tight against her chest.

She isn't what I thought. This isn't his sweetheart. This is his sister. She's waiting at home, watching for him out a picture window in the capital, terrified he'll never return, that her family is fractured forever. The same way those men have fractured mine.

Where are you? Her anguished voice like soft satin torn against the grain. *Come home. Please just come home.*

There are other things I can see too, rising up in my mind uninvited. All the witchfinders, gathered there in the Wharf District of the capital. They chortle in distant taverns, their silver tankards clanging together at the rims, always demanding another round even when they've had more than enough to last a lifetime.

Men like them never know when to stop.

But tonight, I won't listen to their laughter, sharp and cruel as heartbreak. I open my eyes and drop the necklace into the mouth of the bottle. It drifts there in the wine, bobbing for a moment before sinking to the bottom, the chain in a tangle, the locket cracked open, that face still peeking out at me, her eyes cold and accusing.

One more ingredient, and this will be ready. There are so many ways I could conjure this. My mother would have done it differently, that's for sure, with rusted nails instead of pins and piss or blood or boiling oil instead of wine. She had her methods, and nothing less would do.

My mother taught me everything she knew, even though I never asked. She shoved spells in my mouth like plump little candies, and I swallowed them down, one by one. The cloying taste always gagged me, but I never complained. She wouldn't have listened anyhow.

"This will keep you safe," she said, and I tried to believe her.

I tried to keep others safe too. That was why I taught the girls in the forest. I thought if I could share this magic, it wouldn't be so heavy to bear. But it turns out, there's nothing so heavy as the weight of what you never wanted to hold.

I take the pins out of the small box and drop them into the wine, one by one, their sharp ends pricking into the silver chain, driving into the witchfinder, driving him away from us.

"Bind him," I whisper, and it's such a simple invocation, so much simpler than how my mother trained me. The incantations she made me recite always stuck in my throat like phlegm. I never used them in the forest with the others. We would invent our own verses to chant to the birds, to the moon, to each other. Yet even now, my mother's voice still echoes inside me, telling me I'm wrong, that this isn't how I ought to cast a spell.

"You're undisciplined," she used to say. "And reckless. You think those girls won't use your own magic against you?"

I would always shake my head. "I trust them," I'd say. "I trust Anna."

For all the good it did me. Now here I am in the dark, all alone, desperate for time to not repeat itself.

The bottle quivers in my hand, the pins spinning inside, the wine simmering. The spell is almost done, but when I part my lips to finish it, no sound comes out, my mouth dry with the words I haven't spoken, words that seem too inadequate now. This single bottle, binding one witchfinder. It can't possibly make any difference. More men like him could follow, an entire army of them, marching into the village until there's no room left, only cottages and shops and inns stuffed to the brim with witchfinders.

But that hasn't happened, not yet. With the bottle in my front pocket, I slip into my threadbare boots and coat. I'll finish in the forest and bury the bottle as deep as I can, embedding it in the earth. Then the witchfinder will have no choice but to leave us.

Outside, the sun cracks through the clouds. Though it only seemed to last a few minutes, casting this spell took all night. I should have expected that. Time moves differently when you're a witch.

I push between the trees, trying to find a place where the ground has thawed enough to dig. I don't want to venture as far as yesterday. I don't want to end up in the Hyland Forest again.

At the edge of a clearing, I crouch down and press my palms into the earth, the tips of my fingers turning pale with cold. Only then do I see it there on the forest floor. A line of black feathers carefully placed one after another like a trail of bread crumbs. There's someone else here. Someone who can brave the forest the same as a witch.

Someone who's standing right in front of me.

chapter four

I EDGE FORWARD, MY FEET CRACKLING AMONG A SEA OF DEAD LEAVES, BUT IN the haze of the morning, I still can't see the figure clearly. Their cloak is dark, and their back is turned to me. No more than ten paces away, it could be anyone, yet fear rises up inside me as I imagine who it is. That man with his calloused hands, eager to ignite a flame or to wrap gently around a woman's throat.

The rim of the forest shimmers in the sun, and the figure turns toward me, those ruddy cheeks, a curtain of dark hair I recognize.

"Anna?" I speak her name as though I'm not certain it's her, as though I'm not looking right at a face I know so well.

"Odette?" She takes a single step toward me, but even though we're standing so close now, I can't get to her in time. We're nearer to the Hyland Forest than I realized, and the border shifts, just an inch, just enough, so that Anna vanishes inside.

"That isn't fair," I say through gritted teeth, but the woods don't care, especially when I surge forward, slipping back inside, exactly how it wants.

The heat is the first thing I feel, worse than before, stickier and more unforgiving than the swelter of mid-July. The trees have bloomed brighter since yesterday, the flowers growing up in patches knee-high, all the colors a dizzying display. The Hyland Forest is coming alive again, and it craves us more than ever.

In front of me, Anna reaches out her arms like a blindfolded schoolgirl, her fingertips nearly swipe my cheek.

I dodge away from her. "Be careful," I say. "I'm right here."

"Where?" she asks, her voice quivering. She's standing before me, but she can't see me—or anything else. She's lost in plain sight, engulfed in enchantment, this place like a bottomless sea.

"It's all right," I say. "I'll get us out of here. Just listen to my voice."

I start to hum an old lullaby, and Anna follows me, the two of us in step, but another sound threatens to drown me out. It's the forlorn call of the birds, rising up out of nowhere.

"Is that them?" Anna asks, tipping her head to the sky. "Have they finally returned?"

"I hope so," I say, and more than ever, I wish this could be real and not just another trick. Anna always loved the birds as much as I did, maybe even more. We'd call to them together, giggling when they would come and perch on our shoulders and roost in our hair. They'd whisper their secrets to us in a language only we could decipher. They'd warn us of coming storms and tell us which fruits were ripened enough to pick. Afterward, when they would take off back to their nests, she'd collect the fallen feathers from the forest floor. She put them all in a jar and gave them to me.

"To keep them safe," she said, but I knew the real reason. To keep them from her father who would have tossed out any sign of magic he could get his hands on.

The birds' melodies fade away now, and Anna and I keep moving. The trees mirror themselves in a circle around us, the reflection set on keeping us here, the same way it tried to trap me yesterday. But somewhere is the spot where I cracked the spell. That tiny gap should be enough for us to escape. It has to be enough.

I continue humming, and Anna stays near me, all of this feeling again like we're only young girls playing a game. Years ago, there were so many games in the forest with Anna and me and the others, all of us holding hands and conjuring glamours. With magic draped over us like a shroud, we'd skip home at dusk, wearing each other's faces to dinner, waiting to see how long it took our families to notice we weren't ourselves. Sometimes, they'd never catch on, not until the glamour shattered and who we really were would settle over us again. After too many times like that, the parents were more than keen on pulling us apart. Soon, Anna and I watched the other girls our age grow up and get engaged and toss colorful bouquets that we never tried to catch. The world was leaving us behind, but she and I never really minded. After all, there ought to be more than one way for a girl to live.

"It's your fault," Samuel told me one Easter Sunday, a season or two before the witchfinders arrived. "Anna's too busy in that forest to ever bother with a suitor or a wedding or a future."

I only smiled back at him. She and I wouldn't be like the others, and maybe that wasn't such a terrible fate. Beatrix never had a family of her own, and she turned out fine. Better than fine, certainly better than my mother with her temper as ripe and sour as a lemon plucked fresh from the grove.

The forest mutters to us again, and I do my best to ignore its cries. There's a cluster of willows nearby, the air swimming around us, twisting as though it's alive. This is it. I keep humming, louder now, and still blinded, Anna follows my voice. I hold my breath and move through the spot in the trees. The world cracks open, an invisible fog lifting at once.

When we look again, we're standing, dizzy and tired, next to a fence along the road, the Hyland Forest once again spitting us out wherever it chooses.

Her eyes no longer clouded, Anna peers at me and sees me now as though for the first time. "Thank you," she says and reaches out for my hand.

I pull away. "Why are you here?" I ask. "What were you doing in the forest?"

Her face goes gray. "I needed to talk to you," she says and looks down at her hands, fumbling with her paste ring. "That man . . . my cousin. He's arrested Beatrix."

I suddenly can't breathe. "When?"

"At her shop around midnight."

Right after we were together. If I'd lingered with her a moment longer, it could have been me too.

"What can I do?" I ask, a sob lodged in my throat.

"I don't know," Anna says, "but he's preparing the pyre now. She doesn't have much time."

Beatrix, a smile and a remedy always at the ready. Now she needs us. The bottle trembles in my pocket, and I place my hand over it, sensing the power brimming there, everything that's still left undone.

"I need to go," I whisper and start toward the road. As I pass, I see over the fence next to us, and I wheeze out a small gasp. We're at the edge of the graveyard. This is where the Hyland Forest abandoned us.

I look back toward Anna, remembering something. "I didn't think you could come into the woods on your own."

She watches me, her eyes as colorless as a tide pool. "I can't," she says, "not usually. But you left me that trail of feathers, and I followed it."

My body goes cold. "That wasn't me," I say, and together, we gaze back toward the forest. The woods are playing games with us, the same as the children. I only wish I knew the rules too.

Without another word, I head home, the spell still simmering in my pocket. I don't have much time, and everything is different now. Simply sending the witchfinder away won't be enough anymore. Even if I bury this bottle deep, it could take him until tomorrow or longer to leave, and then it will be far too late for Beatrix.

I need something stronger than earth. I need the same weapon these men use against us.

Back at my cottage, the hearth is still flickering from last night. I stand before it, focusing on the flames, drawing them up higher, making them burn brighter. In the corner of the room, the old spells from the other witches whisper louder as though the magic is more restless than before, the lock on the hope chest quivering and swelling and nearly splitting in two.

And there's someone else here as well. The witchfinder's sister, murmuring inside the locket.

Please. That frantic voice that could break a heart in an instant. *Don't hurt him. Just send him back to me.*

I bite my bottom lip to keep myself from sobbing too. "I'm sorry," I say, and before she can speak another word, I toss the bottle into the fire. The glass sizzles against the flames, the pins digging in deeper, the wine swirling darker within. Somewhere, his sister is wailing, even though she doesn't quite know why. She can't see me the same way I can see her, but she understands beyond reason that something is wrong.

I can't think of any of that now. The flames engulfing the bottle, I close my eyes, my mind surging out of the forest and down past the crossroads, darting this way and that along the road until I see him in the town square, his faded jacket pressed, his weathered boots polished. There he is, grinning to himself, masquerading as a gentleman, the pyres all around him like morbid souvenirs of a journey he hasn't taken yet. The specter of my hands extends before me out of the cottage and into the village, ready to wrap around him and make him stop, make all of this stop.

But as my fingers close around him, my whole body goes numb, and nothing happens. He feels nothing, and neither do I. The spell bottle should break when this is done, but there it is in the hearth, intact and gleaming.

My jaw set, I focus again, my hands burning, my muscles turning to stone within me. He's right there, captured in my mind, captured in this bottle, but it makes no difference. Before me, the fire goes out, and when I reach for the bottle, the glass is inexplicably cold in my hand. It won't break, and I know why. We're too far apart for the magic to work. If I want this, I'll have to go to him. Face to face is the only way.

One more trip into that village. Then this will be done.

The town square is teeming with fear, everyone gathering but still keeping their distance from the pyres. My arms crossed, I cut through the crowd, all of them parting around me, terrified to be so close to me, the witch in their midst.

In the center of the throng, Beatrix stands tall like a stoic among the straw, her hands tied tight in a dozen knots. There's a row of pyres around her, the rest of them empty and waiting. The witchfinder hovers near her, testing the rope, beaming when he sees me.

"Hello again," he says and bows his head to me.

I'm exposed out in the open, no more than a few steps away from him. "I don't understand," I say. "What crime did she commit?"

At this, his face contorts, and he gapes at me as though my question is an obscene gesture. "You know what she's done," he says slowly like that's the only way to make me understand. "We all know what she's done."

I look up at Beatrix, and she gazes back at me, something in her eyes soft and reassuring. Even now, she's the one comforting me.

"You're wrong," I whisper to him, my throat raw. "She's a healer, not a witch."

He tilts his head, one eyebrow twitching up. "What's the difference?" he asks, and for a moment, I wonder if he really doesn't know, if maybe I could explain this to him. Then a thin smirk blossoms on his lips, and he grips the flint and iron tighter in his hand, ready to strike the flame. A heavy wave of nausea ripples through me, and I realize it doesn't matter. I could explain everything to him, but he'll burn her anyway.

The spell aches in my fingertips, but his sister's voice rises up in my mind again, those anguished cries, and I hesitate, wanting to try one last time to reason with him.

"Go back," I say, steeling myself against him. "Your sister needs you at home."

His face shifts, his gentleman's facade melting away as he glares into me. "And what exactly do you know of my sister?"

"That she's waiting for you," I say. "Go to her. *Please.*"

"No," he says, his jaw clenched. "You don't know about her. That means you don't get to speak of her."

He moves nearer to me now, and my lips part, desperate to call up the spells I've been taught. Yet all I can expel is a guttural moan, an invocation all tangled in on itself. It's only part of the magic and not nearly enough to make a difference. After everything, I can't finish this.

And I've run out of time. With a final step, this man closes the distance between us. I try to holler out anything—a spell, a scream, a swear—but he takes hold of me, a mistake he doesn't realize he's making until it's too late.

One touch and the heat of my flesh sears right through him.

Smoke rising from his scorched fingers, he screams out, and I wrench away, stumbling backward toward the crowd. Once again, they part around me. This is the reason everyone in the village knows to keep their distance from me. The last pyres in this square might have burned out years ago, but I didn't. The fire lives in me now, this eternal burning that will never let me forget, never let me move on, never let me be close to anyone again, not without my body singeing through them.

His hand blackened, the man stumbles in a dizzied circle before he catches himself and twists toward me, marveling at me like I'm a specimen in a curiosity cabinet.

"It's you," he says, his eyes flickering with mad glee. "You're the one."

The one he's been searching for. The witch they couldn't burn. In the capital, they must tell their urban legends about me, the heretic who wouldn't die, and he knows what that means—my execution will be sacrosanct. It will give him power and respect, will make him a bona fide witchfinder. The only thing standing between him and his destiny is my beating heart.

I back away, trying to coax this magic out of me, to speak the words my mother taught me, to utter anything at all, but I'm frozen. The witchfinder, however, is ready. He unsheathes his knife, the blade curved and rusted and glistening with thick oil. Henbane probably, just to make a wound more agonizing if you dare survive the initial blow. He inches toward me, one careful step at a time as though I'm a scared rabbit who might bolt. I stare into him, still struggling to speak when Anna's voice rises up behind me.

"Leave her alone."

She's pushed to the front of the crowd even as Samuel tries to hold her back, pitifully bleating her name.

"Anna, please," he says, reaching for her, but she's already broken away from him, headed toward the witchfinder.

"Stop all of this," she says, this one final plea to her cousin, her kin.

But he only guffaws, thick spit clinging to the corners of his mouth. "Go home, Anna," he says. "Make this easier on both of us."

He turns back to me, knife ready, prepared to finish me right here in the street, no fire needed, but Anna's too quick for him. She cuts between me and the witchfinder, and he brings down the knife, aiming for me but slashing at her arm instead. She cries out, her hands clawing at his face. With fury bubbling inside him, he takes hold of her by the wrist, her blood slick against his flesh.

"So you're in league with the devil too?" he asks, dipping his face closer to hers.

She bares her teeth at him, a feral animal, the same girl I remember from long ago. "Better than being in league with you."

The witchfinder raises his knife again, his eyes glinting, and though Anna looks ready to go for his throat, she won't make it. That blade will plunge into her first, straight through her heart, and no spell on earth will be able to reverse it.

I won't watch her die.

I won't watch this cycle repeat itself.

I step forward, my gaze set squarely on him, and this time, I forget everything I've been taught, every word my mother forced into my mouth, every doubt she sowed in me.

"No," I say, my voice swelling with rage, and this single word is enough. Something tears inside me, like the ripping of old canvas. It's coming now, the memory of the flames that burned all the witches to nothing, their screams that still echo through my own bones.

His face blanching daisy white, the man senses the spell stirring inside him. I sense it inside me too, like bubbles bursting in my blood. It puts things in my mind that were never there before. A thousand gruesome images, all of them flaring at once inside me.

A clean slash of a throat in the dark. A twig-snap of a neck. A smear of red, coughed up in a tattered handkerchief. Burnt flesh, eviscerated flesh, flesh that melts and sizzles and withers from the bone.

The spell is giving me the choice: how I want this man to end. Until this instant, I never realized just how many ways there are to die.

I turn away and focus on here, on now. Anna and Beatrix and this stone beneath my feet. I have to keep myself grounded in this moment, or I'll be lost in it. Let the spell decide for itself how it wants to finish. I won't choose. I won't become like him—another common murderer.

The witchfinder still can't fathom what I've done. He stumbles toward me, his eyes spiderwebbed with red. "Tomorrow," he murmurs. "I'll finish you tomorrow."

He drifts back and forth, villagers inching away on all sides, before he finally collapses with an agonizing thud at our feet. For a long minute, we listen quietly as he convulses and keens, the magic sinking into his flesh like rusted fishing hooks.

His brow twisted, Samuel hovers near Anna, his hands wrapped tight around her arm, stymieing the bleeding. "The cut's not too bad," he says, and I wonder how he can be so certain.

The villagers start to disperse, but Samuel cuts them off first.

"We can't leave him like this," he says, looking wildly around the crowd. "We need to take him somewhere to rest, somewhere for treatment. The tavern maybe?"

The owner shakes his head. "I won't have a witchfinder in my establishment."

I almost laugh aloud at this. Even an hour ago, he'd have given this man a room. He'd have given him anything he asked for. All of the villagers would have. But things have changed now that the witchfinder is twitching in a pool of blood and enchantment. They scoff at what remains of him before turning away, leaving us to clean up a mess we all share. Everyone can afford to have courage once courage is no longer needed.

Only a few of the women remain, the ones that used to dance in the forest with Anna and me. The clerk from the general store, the blacksmith's wife, the schoolteacher. With gentle hands, they unknot the ropes that bind Beatrix's body, and they help her down from the pyre.

"We'll take care of her," the schoolteacher says to me, and together, they lead Beatrix home, their arms wrapped around her, guiding the way.

Now the square's nearly deserted, leaving only Anna, Samuel, and me to pick up the pieces of the witchfinder. This man, fancying himself omnipotent only a few moments ago, lies curled up like a limp fish at our feet. I remind myself he would have done so much worse to us if he'd had the chance. The spell curdles in my stomach, and I want to go home now. That's all I've wanted for days.

"Why not just abandon him?" I whisper, but Samuel tosses me a hideous grimace over his shoulder.

"He's family," he says with a grunt. "You don't leave family to die in the street."

"They left mine to die," I say. Samuel doesn't hear me. Instead, he motions to Anna, and the two of them lift up the burbling witchfinder and carry him home. Anna's still bleeding, and now she's expected to help the man who did it to her.

A few steps behind, I follow, unable to help her, unable to do much of anything. In a way, I suppose I've already done more than enough.

A hurricane lamp flickers in the window of their cottage, and they tuck the witchfinder in bed like a groggy child. I linger at the front door, away from them, wavering halfway between here and not here, but I'm still not alone. There's a whispering in my pocket and the gentle rhythm of faraway sobs. I remove the bottle from my jacket and gaze into the open locket, drifting in dark wine, the girl's face contorted in agony. Somewhere, she knows. Though she can't entirely understand it, she can feel what I've done to him.

Wheezing, Anna returns from the bedroom and collapses in her father's rocking chair, the edges of her cut already glistening yellow. "How long?" she asks. "Until the spell's over?"

She turns her eyes on me, and she's not the only one watching. Samuel has emerged from the bedroom as well, and the two of them are waiting, wanting to know about what I've done, how it works.

I slip the bottle back in my coat where the cries will go unanswered. "I don't know."

"About what?" Samuel scowls, the corners of his mouth twitching. "About how long? Or about what happens?"

"About any of it," I say.

"What do you mean?" He stares at me. "How many times have you done this?"

"None," I say, and the word sticks in my throat like a glob of glue. "I've never cursed anyone before."

chapter five

THE ROOM RETREATS TO A SULLEN SILENCE, ANNA AND SAMUEL BOTH understanding it at the same time. That I'm not what they thought. The witch they believed could unravel the whole village hasn't cursed so much as a flea.

This isn't the first time I've tried. Five years ago, when the men descended on us, thick as a colony of red ants, my mother made me try, her daughter with the uncanny gift. A spell with jagged edges that was supposed to send the witchfinders away, bind them up with their own power, save us all from their wrath. But all I managed to do was to spook a few of the men's horses. The witchfinders never even knew they'd been cursed. Meanwhile, the incantation left me in bed for a week, a sharp ache in my bones right down to the marrow, head heavy as a stone.

"Don't worry," my mother whispered, keeping vigil over my sickbed. "We'll try again when you're well."

But I wasn't sure there was enough left in me to try again. Certainly not to try alone. That's because there was something else that my mother never taught me, something I had to figure out on my own: that hexes are ugly business. The way they lodge beneath the skin like a thorn, twisting deeper every time you try to root them out. When it's all over, a witch too often wishes she'd learned to let go rather than hold on so tight.

Only the witchfinders didn't give me a choice. I had to do something today, even if I can't be sure what will become of me because of it.

"You must have some idea about how all this works," Samuel keeps insisting. "How long do you think until it's done?"

As in until the witchfinder is dead. Except Samuel won't use that word. He won't admit aloud what I've done, what he wanted me to do. People are so brave until they have to confront ugly things with their own eyes.

"There's no way to be sure," I say, my hands trembling in front of me. "Might be a week. Or a month. Or maybe it'll be over in an hour."

"So you don't know anything?" Samuel asks, disgust flushing his cheeks, and I gnaw my bottom lip, wishing I wasn't here. I don't belong in this house that's hanging onto its pain as tightly as I do. I start to move through the door, back toward the street, but Anna looks to me, the color leeching from her face.

"Please," she whispers, and I know immediately what she means.

Don't leave us with him. Not until this is finished.

I breathe deep and gaze out the window. I'll stay, not just for her but because I don't have any other choice. Outside, the afternoon has gotten away from us. Days keep doing that to me—vanishing before I've a chance to hold them in my hand. It will be dark soon, and the shadows are probably already on their way to me.

"Salt," I whisper. "I need salt."

Samuel hesitates, not entirely certain he wants to help a witch. "In the kitchen," he says finally.

Back out in the cold, I pour a thick circle around the house, careful that the line remains unbroken. From behind the windows in nearby houses, the other villagers watch me. They don't understand what I'm doing, how this salt is for what's coming, for the things they never prepare for. Things that witches have to stop instead.

When I return inside, Anna and Samuel are in the bedroom with the witchfinder again, their voices seeping through the closed door.

"It won't hurt anything," Anna is saying.

"After what she's done—"

"You mean saving our lives?"

"That remains to be seen."

"I don't care. I'm taking it to her," she says and throws open the door. I back away half-startled, and when she sees me, she does her best to smile.

"This is for you," she says and passes me a small bowl. It's the leftover soup from yesterday, the meal she was cooking when the witchfinder arrived. Anna knows how tired I am, how starving too, my ribs peeking through my skin, my belly gnawing at itself.

I hold the bowl in both hands and swallow the salted broth down in one gulp.

"Thank you," I whisper, and Anna is about to say something else when Samuel comes out of the bedroom, cursing under his breath.

"He's resting now," he says to us as though it matters, as though a night's sleep will be enough to change anything. Samuel locks the bedroom door behind him and deposits the key in his desk drawer in the corner. It's the same desk where he used to sit down and compose his poison pen letters to the village.

The meat was cold, the bread was stale, he'd send off to the tavern, his correspondence as bitter and regular as Sunday Mass.

The grain has gone pink, he'd write to the general store whether it was true or not. *And now thanks to you, my horse has colic.*

My favorites were the ones he would send to my mother. The grievances were different each time—I'd made Anna late for Christmas Eve dinner, or I'd filled her pockets with salt and ruined her best dress, or I'd simply dared to exist—but the parting line was always the same.

Tell your wicked daughter to leave my girl alone or else.

My mother never bothered to open the letters. She gave them to me instead as though my name was on the envelope and not hers.

"There's no point in that family," she would say. "I don't know why you bother with that girl."

Because we're alike, I wanted to say, and I wonder if that's still true.

Samuel shoves the desk drawer closed, muttering to himself, the years receding on his face, leaving all the bitterness behind but not much more. Without a word, he lumbers off to sleep in his room, but Anna, evicted from her own bed, curls up with a ragged blanket in the rocking chair next to the hearth. She's wounded and needs rest, but her own father let the witchfinder have her bedroom.

"Why do you stay?" I ask even though I know I shouldn't. Even though it's a cruel question.

Anna shrugs, drawing the blanket tighter around her. "There's nowhere else for women like us to go, Odette. You know that."

I draw in a sharp breath, hating how much she's right. These days, every time I catch my reflection in a glimmer of glass or a silvery mud puddle, I think how I'm too old now to be a maiden, too young to be a crone, never wanted to become a mother. There's no place in the world for a woman like me. Even if I wasn't a witch, the villagers wouldn't know what to do with me.

Anna understands this. Maybe she and I are still the same.

A murmur through the door, and we both look toward the witchfinder, imagining him there in bed, dreaming his restless dreams.

"Did your cousin ever say why he came, to this place in particular?" I look to her. "Or why he's back now?"

Anna shakes her head. "He never mentioned a word to me."

"How about your father? Does he know?"

"Not that he's told me," she says.

Maybe they don't know because there isn't a good reason. I pull my knees into my chest and rest in the window seat, the cold leaking through the glass.

Anna smiles a little to herself. "This is almost like before," she says. Back when we were girls, she means, when the world seemed different somehow. Anna and I used to giggle and pretend we didn't hear Samuel, no matter how loudly he bellowed. Right here at this hearth, she and I would play together, making shadow puppets on the wall. Sometimes, my sister Freya would join in too, all of us contorting our fingers to make different shapes of monsters in the gloom.

"We should run away," Freya would say, giving us that crooked smile of hers. "Then we could do this all the time."

That was my sister's answer to everything—escape. She thought running could fix any problem. Freya always had big dreams, and none of them involved this village.

"Someday we'll go to the capital," she'd say, her face brightening because that was back in a world before the witchfinders, before we had to be so afraid. "The capital is where all the other witches are, Odette. They have everything there. Towering buildings and ballrooms and an apothecary chock-full of magic." She'd suck air through her teeth, savoring the visions in her head. "With all those ingredients, we could bless the whole world." Then she'd grin at me. "Or curse it."

But for all her talk of other witches, my sister wasn't like me. She never made friends the way I tried to, and she never took to magic either. Sure, she could conjure a glamour here and there but almost nothing else. That was why our mother didn't bother much with her, instead focusing her energy into me.

Situated before the hearth, our mother would hold me in her arms, gripping me so tight I could barely breathe.

"Make the flame dance, Odette," she'd whisper, the scents of jasmine and sandalwood on her skin.

I'd fidget and hide my face. "I don't want to."

"Come on now," she'd say. "Just a little. Just show me you're a good girl."

At night, Freya and I would curl up together in our sagging bed, our secrets beneath us, tucked away. Her maps of faraway places and Anna's jar of feathers. If our mother caught us with either, we'd earn a dozen lashes.

"You don't have to do what Mama tells you," Freya would whisper, and I'd nod as though I believed her. As though I had a choice.

So I did something else. When our mother wasn't looking, I poured a ring of salt around the house. This one wasn't for ghosts—it was for men. To cast out anyone who intended us harm. My gift to our mother, the only spell I ever did for her without her asking. For all the good it did us.

In the rocking chair, Anna dozes off, but I stay awake, waiting for the darkness. It will come. I know that already. We make it almost to midnight, my head heavy, before the rapping arrives at the window.

Anna's eyes flick open. "Who is it?" she asks, her voice as thin as spider thread, clutching the hem of the blanket, her knuckles clenched white.

"It's all right," I whisper. "Go back to sleep. I'll keep watch."

And I'll keep them out. Every murmur of a ghost, every labored creak like the lurching of wagon wheels, every melody that could be the lost birds or could just be the wind. My fingers pressed against the glass, I try to push away the world, but my hands ache, twitching and alive with power. The tug of the shadows is always sweeter than I remember it, like a smooth sip of mulberry wine on an August afternoon. It makes me want to leave, to swing open that front door and waltz all the way to the graveyard. That's where I belong. I should have been there five years ago, buried deep alongside my parents. Maybe that's why I keep returning there, night after night. Because it already feels like home.

In the pocket of my jacket, shoved beneath the bottle, is the red ribbon that Beatrix gave me from her shop. I wrench it out and steady myself by tying a knot. Then I tie another one. The whir of phantoms is like honeybees outside the window, and I keep my hands occupied.

Anna drifts back to sleep, a light fever seeping into her, her arm wrapped up in a piece of an old gingham dress. That wound is getting worse. I can see that even from here.

I tie another knot, tighter this time. She'll be all right. That's what I promise myself. But then I've promised myself a lot of things that haven't come true. Like escaping what came before, these memories I can't shake. Even now, there's someone else in the room, floating all around us, that rich voice from the capital that never stops searching for me.

Come to me, Odette. His sharp laugh, thick and thoroughbred yet greasy too. *I'm waiting.*

"And you'll wait a whole lot longer," I whisper and continue looping the ribbon again and again until my vision blurs and sleep comes whether I like it or not.

I awaken in the morning, choking up screams that aren't my own. At first, I don't remember where I am, but the smudges like tiny fingerprints on the other side of the window help to remind me.

Nearby, Anna is sitting on the floor outside the bedroom, her ear pressed against the locked door.

"He hasn't stirred since before dawn," she says, "since before I woke up."

Together, we peer beneath the door, but it's dark inside, all the curtains drawn.

"Do you think it's over?" Anna asks, her eyes wide and hopeful.

"Maybe," I say, but we need to know for sure. Anna understands this. Her steps quiet as a ghost's, she creeps over to her father's desk and retrieves the key from the drawer. Her fingers shaking, she brings it to me, and with the metal cold in my hand, I unlock the door.

It creaks open toward us, revealing only more shadow, our eyes taking a moment to adjust before we see it—the outline of a man who seems so much larger than before, his body right there in the doorway, blotting out the light. He moves forward, and I'm suddenly only a hairsbreadth away from a witchfinder, his breath heavy and stinking with phlegm and yesterday's gruel. He must have been standing there, motionless on the other side for hours, waiting for us to open the door, his patience limitless and unfathomable.

"Good morning, Odette." His pale lips curl into a grotesque grin. "You'll have that meal with us now."

Leering over me, he stumbles forward, sweaty and hulking, and I gag down air, backing away—my feet in a tangle beneath me—until I'm leaned up against the table on the other side of the room. The magic rises up in me again, spiraling before my eyes like a nightmare or a dream. The witchfinder's fingers twitch toward his belt, a knife still sheathed there, and with rage scorching inside me, I move a little closer to him, my body its own weapon. My touch will be enough to make him scream, the same way he'd like to hear me scream. I reach out toward him, and his eyes widen, daring me to try it, but Anna is hovering next to us now like an intrusive mother.

"Enough of that," she says. "Please sit, both of you. I'll get us breakfast."

She waits a moment until we each withdraw, the witchfinder to the hearth and me to the window. Then she moves toward the kitchen to make good on her promise. Anna still wants to see this end well, but the only happy ending is a quick one. I should finish this right now. Only I'm not even sure how to do that. I could grab hold of him, tight as a thumbscrew, but he'll simply cut off my hand and maybe Anna's too, just to prove a point.

If only this magic would hurry up. If only this could be done already.

Samuel appears in the doorway of his bedroom, sleep clogging the corners of his eyes, always a minute late enough to avoid any real trouble. He looks from me to the witchfinder and back again, and he seems almost ready to say something when Anna returns from the kitchen, a heavy cast-iron pot in her arms. I move to help her with it, but she waves me off.

"Take your seats," she commands us, and we do as she says because even enemies have to eat. The four of us gather around the table, ladling thin oatmeal from the pot, one after another. Everyone is careful to keep their distance from me, their hands never brushing against mine, even though the witchfinder wants to be closer than ever. He watches me, the glint in his eyes promising me the same thing over and over. *I'll finish you.*

My guts twist with the reflection of this spell, with the residual of what I've done to him. He might be right except not in the way he thinks. I try not to look at him, but he grimaces at me, gripping his spoon tighter as though it's my throat. His bones shift a little beneath his skin, everything in him shifting, though he doesn't seem to notice.

"It's so nice to finally meet, Odette," he says. "I've heard so many things about you."

I stare at him, his face swirling gray with the magic I put there. "And who exactly is talking about me?"

"You know who," he says, and at once, that rich voice is ringing again in my head as inescapable as the summer sun.

Samuel shovels down another mouthful of oatmeal. "Can we please have breakfast in peace?" he asks, and the witchfinder lets out a blistering laugh.

"Ask the witch," he mumbles. "She's causing all this trouble."

I grit my teeth. "I'm not the one who came to this village ready to set it on fire."

The witchfinder sneers at me, his lips twitching into an almost-smile, but something in his face pales at once, and the whole room seizes up. Anna's fingers knot into weak fists, and Samuel chokes up a small wheeze, both of them waiting, watching.

I look down, hoping silently that maybe the spell is almost done. Maybe this curse is nearly over. But as the witchfinder's thin hands fumble for his own throat, I already know this magic is just getting started.

He stumbles to his feet, the table swaying against his weight, his body drifting back and forth until he folds at the waist, his filmy gaze set on me. His face shifts again, and I try not to scream as he chokes up blood and pus and something else, something dark. It plops onto the table in a pool of crimson and oatmeal. A long, twisted piece of rusted metal.

And he's not done yet. Gagging again, he brings up another one and another after that. It's not until there are a dozen of them lined up in front of us that I realize what they are.

Coffin nails. The witchfinder is retching up coffin nails.

Anna covers her mouth with both hands, turning away. We all ate from the same pot, which means this wasn't her work. This was because of me. It doesn't matter that I never imagined this or willed it to be. Instead, this spell is taking on a mind of its own.

The witchfinder thrashes against the table, all of our bowls overturning in our laps, colorless slop leaking down our legs.

He staggers back toward the bedroom, toward where he'll be alone.

"I'll burn you at sundown," he slurs at me.

"No," I say, and regret coils inside me. "You won't."

With his flesh drooping from his bones, I doubt he'll make it to evening.

The door slams behind him, and the three of us are left at the ruined table.

Of course, maybe I'm wrong. Maybe the witchfinder will make it to evening. He could hold on like this for weeks. All because of me, all because I'm stuck.

The spell is only halfway there. I can't decide, so neither will the magic. I've wished all day long to curse these men, but now that I've gotten my chance, I can't follow through. It's easier to banish someone in my mind than with these hands, these words, this heart.

I glance at Anna's arm, the wound festering around the edges, her thick bandages soaked through in the night. "You need stitches," I whisper.

She shakes her head. "I'm fine," she says and gathers up our bowls. "Everything's fine."

Anna bolts for the kitchen, trying not to wince as she shoves open the door. It won't be long until the infection is so much worse than that.

"We need to help her," I say, and Samuel nods.

"I'll fetch the doctor." He pushes back his chair, eager for any excuse to get away from this table. In a flash, he's out the door, leaving me alone to listen to the gurgling from the bedroom. The jarring noise is like a dull blade dragged across my skin. The magic boils up inside me, wanting to be finished, wanting to live forever. Part of every spell demands to go on, to never end, so it can stay inside you, wriggling beneath your ribs like a hungry worm.

This shouldn't all be on me. The villagers could finish this too. The witchfinder is weakened now, which would make it easy. A tea to coax him into a dreamless sleep, a knife in the back, a brick to the head. If the others want him gone, they could do it themselves. But I already know what their answer would be.

"That's murder," they'd say as if what I'm doing is any different. They don't care what will become of me, how I don't want this on my conscience either. I don't want to be like those men. Once you've ended a life, it never goes away. There's no expiration on it, no moment when your slate is wiped clean. All I've ever wanted was for these men to stop. That's just never been a choice they've given us.

A chill piercing though me, I'd prefer to sleep and let this day wash away from me, but I'm not so lucky. Samuel materializes again at the front door, his face pale as clotted cream.

"The doctor won't come," he says and glares at the bedroom door where the witchfinder is grumbling in the dark. "Not so long as he's here."

I close my eyes and try not to scream. Of course, the doctor won't help. Nobody in this village will help us with a witchfinder in the house. Nobody except for one person.

"Beatrix," I say. "She'll know what we need."

I struggle to my feet, but aching and numb, I collapse back toward the table, my body too worn down from the spell. I don't want to send Samuel to her. I don't trust him when it comes to things like this. Folk remedies and herbs with names he can't or won't pronounce. He treats everything he doesn't understand like it's an affront to him, a personal insult.

I try again to stand, but Samuel just shakes his head and holds up one hand. "I'll go," he says, and before I can argue, he vanishes, leaving me on my own again. Anna hasn't returned from the kitchen, and I wonder if she's curled up on the butcher block, napping among the smears of lard and flour, the oatmeal already crusting along the rims of the soiled breakfast bowls. She'll seize any chance to rest today, to sleep off the sickness already seeping through her.

That leaves me alone, one room away from a witchfinder.

Then I'm no longer a room away. I'm standing over his bed, staring down at him. For a moment, I don't know how I got here, but then I realize it. The spell—it's guiding me. It's bubbling through my veins, giving me the choice, reminding me I need to finish this. I need to decide how this ends. Only I don't want to choose. I don't want to be the one who stops his heart with my own hands.

I close my eyes, and his sister's voice is suddenly in the room with us.

I'll tell you. Her words lilting like a forgotten lullaby. *I'll tell you all about the man you're murdering.*

My breath heaving, I take out the bottle and look at the locket inside. The girl gazes up at me, alive in a way only a picture can be. Her lips move silently, but I hear her all the same.

He's afraid. Her voice no more than a whisper. *Of being nothing, of being forgotten.*

There's a deep groan in his belly, and the witchfinder's eyes open. I start to back away, but he's already looking right into me.

"You did this." He says it almost as a question, as though he still can't believe it's true. Part of him probably never thought there were any real witches in the world.

I shake my head. "I never meant for it to happen like this."

His hands reach out blindly for me, and he nearly swipes at my arm. "But it was you?"

"Yes," I say.

He rolls to one side, sweat draping his brow, a gnat in the corner of his eye. "I'll die here, won't I?"

"Yes." I almost say I'm sorry, but I know it's not true, so I say nothing at all.

His hand trembling, he reaches out and takes hold of my hem, the closest he can get to me, the closest I can get to anyone.

"Do you think I'll go to heaven?" he asks, and the question hits me hard in the chest.

"No, sir," I say, not looking at him. "I don't."

He hesitates. "What if I repent?"

My eyes flick up at him. "What if you recover?"

In the waning light of afternoon, I stare at him, and he stares back, and we understand each other for the first time. How all the contrition in the world will amount to nothing if his fever breaks. If this man stands strong again, he'll still execute the women among us. Even if I reverse this curse, he'll still execute me.

"Odette?" Samuel is standing behind me, his steps so quiet that I never heard him come in. "Beatrix is here. And she'll only talk to you."

I turn away and leave him alone with the witchfinder.

Beatrix falters at the front door, never passing the threshold. She's like the rest: too superstitious to enter this home right now.

I join her in the alley, our shadows long between the narrow houses.

She drops a vial of ointment into my hand. "For Anna," she says and hesitates. "And the witchfinder?"

"Still here," I say.

"You never used to be so afraid of magic."

"I never used to visit everyone I ever loved in the cemetery."

"Not everyone," she says. "I hear your sister made it to the capital."

I grunt. "Freya could have made it to hell for all I care."

Beatrix flashes me a grin. "She's probably been there too. Took a detour on her way out of town."

At this, I exhale a sharp laugh, the first time in too long. I don't even mean it about my sister. I only hate her because I miss her so much. But it's nice to laugh, and it's nice to see Beatrix smile again too. She starts to say something else, but time splits in two, a scream within the house shattering the day.

I stumble inside, Beatrix right behind me, and we see it at the same instant. The witchfinder has limped from his bed. He stands in the middle of the room, clinging to Anna, his hands sliding all over her body, his clumsy fingers splaying on her throat, across her mouth, his nails digging into the gaping wound on her arm. She cries out again, an agonizing wail, but he doesn't let go. He knows that, unless he can stop me, this is the final moment before all his other moments will be erased. His last chance to do something, to prove something.

My last chance too. If I can't stop him, he's liable to snap her thin neck with his bare hands or smother her against his chest. Or maybe he'll invent a new way to murder a girl. The witchfinders are good at that.

In my jacket, the locket whispers again to me, telling me about him, what he fears, this man who wants to be everything in the world at once.

He's afraid of being forgotten, his sister says, and this time, I listen. The shadows twisting and contorting all around the room, I hold my breath and conjure it inside me.

"Be nothing," I whisper, and when I exhale, the end of the spell unfurls from me, not in words spoken aloud but in darkness. It's all smoke and stench and cruel laughter that cuts deeper than any blade. Instantly the spell bottle shatters in my pocket, leaking red down my body, and the enchantment surrounds him, finishing what I couldn't do only yesterday.

Even after everything, it takes longer than I expect. It starts with a moan from deep in his belly and a weak fist extended to no one in particular. Anna breaks away from him as his legs wobble and his pants bloom bright yellow, the color of fresh butter on a supper table. He doesn't fall at first. His body is still fighting to live, though somewhere in his mind he knows it's already too late.

Then the way he crumples up like crushed paper beneath a heavy boot makes everything in me shake. My lips part to scream, to take it all back, to make it go quicker, but this is it. The spell is done. All I can do is wait for it to be over.

On the floor, he has no shape, only a vague outline of a useless body. Twitching on his formless belly, he crawls a few inches and stops and then crawls a little farther before he can't move anymore, before he'll never move again. Nearby, Anna exhales a small whimper as Beatrix grips her hand, and they shudder together side by side. This isn't what they wanted. It's not what anyone wanted. This was supposed to be quick, easy. Not some messy spectacle that reminds us how ugly death can be.

I reach out to steady myself, but there's nothing to hold onto. Just the darkness of a room where I don't belong.

A burble from the pit of his knotted-up guts—and the rest of him withers before our eyes. His skin turns to clay on his bones, and the clay gives way to ash. His face is the last to disintegrate, the eyes sinking into the dark, so deep in the sockets I don't know where they go. He tries once more to cry out, but his lips droop and crust over, his cheeks crumbling apart like a slice of week-old cake.

Anything resembling him is gone in an instant. All that's left fades into nothing on the hardwood floor, a pile of thick dust slipping between the cracks and knotholes, disappearing as though he were never here at all.

The room spins around me, and I rasp out a wheeze, my skin suddenly too heavy for my own body. Next to me, Anna lets out a single cry, her throat raw with grief.

"Is it over?" she asks through bitter tears.

"Yes," I say as the ceiling tilts, and I collapse to the floor among the ash.

chapter six

THEIR SCREAMS STARTLE ME AWAKE, THE SAME SCREAMS THAT NEVER STOP echoing inside me. This strident melody of ragged cries and restless flames and the drip-drop of melted skin puddling into the cracks of the earth.

I try to scream too, but my mouth is clogged and raw as if packed with dirt. A thrash of wings in the distance—and my eyes snap open, the world seeping back in, my family's voices receding around me. Then I have to remember all over again that they're not here anymore. They haven't been for a long time.

It was just another bad dream. That's all. Curled in bed, I do my best to drift back asleep, but when I roll over, something pierces my flesh. My fingers quivering, I pluck it from the inside of my thigh.

A coffin nail.

This isn't the forest. This isn't my cottage. I'm still at Samuel and Anna's house, still in this room where the witchfinder tried and failed to recuperate. A place where I don't belong.

There's a single window at the end of the bed, a ribbon of light leaking through. It's a way out, a way to freedom, but as I rise up toward it, nausea ripples through me, and my muscles go slack. Head fevered, I'm nearly dreaming, even though I'm wide awake.

This is all left over from the spell, from what I did to that man who's no more. This ache that feels like it belongs to me now, like I might never shake what I've done.

"Odette?" Beatrix is standing in the doorway, her slight frame backlit, making her appear more shadow than flesh. "Can you hear me?"

My mouth slips open, and I try to answer her, I try to ask for her help, but the words wither on my lips.

"It's all right," she whispers. "I've got something for that."

Shuffling to the bed, she leans over me, her face lined, careful never to let her skin touch mine. A bent spoon dipped in the ointment, she slathers thick goo down my neck and chest. An expectorant. My lungs release at once, phlegm rising up the back of my throat. I wilt over the side of the bed and heave up flecks of brown and yellow and spring green, thin strings of it sticking to the corners of my mouth. Still heaving, I gulp down air, reminding myself I'm here, I'm still alive. The witchfinders haven't done me in yet. My own magic hasn't done me in.

As I'm drooping over the mattress, something catches my eye, no more than a yard from the edge of the bed. The crow curled up and quiet as though he's only sleeping, his beak still split, his wings still broken.

"He just showed up this morning," Beatrix says, her curious gaze fixed on the body.

I glance about the room. There are no gaps in the corners, no cracks in the walls, no shattered glass anywhere. The crow should have had no way in, but here he is anyhow, my constant companion, his slick feathers glinting in the barest of sunlight. He isn't lost to the forest after all.

Beatrix moves toward the doorway, turning back once. "Do you want me to take care of him?" she asks.

"No," I say, my throat thick with bile. "Please leave him."

I want the crow with me, this strange creature who's come back to watch over me.

Nodding, Beatrix shuts the door behind her, and with the sweat-stained mattress sagging beneath me, I close my eyes and drift away, dreaming of birds, their wings smooth, their immaculate flight taking them anywhere but here. Maybe even taking me with them.

I look again, and it's hours later, the sun faded from the sky, a new visitor outside the window.

Through the smudged glass, the little girl beams at me. "Are you dead yet?"

I shake my head. "Sorry," I say.

"That's all right." She grins at me. "You'll get there eventually. We all do."

My belly soured, I try again to sit up, but my muscles go slack. I'm stuck in this moment, in this bed. No way home, no way out of the village.

The bedroom door is closed, but someone is right there on the other side, hovering near the hearth. I listen for a voice, hoping it's Anna, but the shadow moves away. I don't blame her if she's angry at me. First the witchfinder stole her bedroom, and now I have. It makes me feel like I'm no different from these men, always pushing into places I don't belong. No wonder I'm alone.

Or mostly alone. The little girl stares up at me through the window, flashing me that gap-toothed grin.

My vision pinwheels at the edges, darkness pressing in. "Who are you?"

She snaps her tongue. "Don't you know my name?"

"Why should I?" My head lolls back against a stiff pillow. "You never introduced yourself."

"Maybe I did," she says brightly. "Maybe you just don't remember."

I exhale a thin laugh. As though I could forget her and her friends. Especially when all around the house, I hear them. The rhythm of tiny bare feet and the creaking of their rusted wagon.

"They want to see you again," the little girl says, and a chorus of giggles leaks into the room.

"Not now," I whisper, my body going numb, but they don't listen. The other children are at the window, peering over the sill, their gazes milky white.

The windowpane bows inward, their fingers pressed against the outside of the glass. Fear surging through me, I contort against the mattress, my hands curled around the headboard, but I'm still not strong enough to stand. And I'll need to run if I want to escape them.

The little girl scowls. "Not yet," she says and pushes the others away. "Don't take it too far, or you'll ruin the game."

The children's faces swirl before me, their eyes shifting colors from gray to blue to black. Then one by one, they turn away, receding from the glass.

The room settles around me, and I put my back to the window. "You're not even really here," I say. "None of you are."

Behind me, a small crystalline giggle. "Then we don't need to worry about leaving."

I shiver, wanting to scream, but right now, I can barely move. The fever burns bright inside me like a dying star, and all at once, everything in the universe goes black.

My sister Freya running, her footfalls heavy as a steed's on the earth.

"Come with me." Her voice an echo, rising up out of the past. That night five years ago, the evening that everything ended. This loop that repeats in my head as though someday I'll be able to reach out and wipe the memory right out of existence.

She and I weren't there when the witchfinders raided the house. Freya had gone wandering like she often did, and I was with Anna in the forest, searching for the birds, certain if only we could find them, it would make all the difference.

"They'll come back," Anna kept promising me. "I know they will."

Not that it could have possibly mattered by then, not when the men had already come for me. They hadn't realized I wasn't home. All they knew was that my house was impenetrable, the protection spell around it strong enough to keep them out, this gift I'd given my mother. The witchfinders couldn't cross the threshold to arrest my family, so they did the next best thing. They burned the whole place down. By the time Freya and I got back, the fire had already gone out. We missed them by hours, our chance to save our mother and father, to do anything at all.

My wail ricocheted off the sky, and I collapsed at the threshold, the ash of our parents lilting in the air. I wouldn't move, not until Freya yanked me to my feet, dragging me out of town, away from the witchfinders who'd heard my cries and had already rounded up their horses to chase me down.

"Please, Odette," she said, trying to entwine her fingers with mine, but I wrenched away from her at the crossroads.

"I won't run," I said, tears soaking my cheeks. "I won't be a coward."

"And I won't end up dead."

She asked me once more to come with her, but I stood there on the road, stubborn to the last, and watched her leave.

The men got hold of me the very next morning. Their hands greasy, they tied me to the pyre and lit the flame, the lonesome stench of brimstone the only last rites they offered me. I screamed so many names—for my sister, my mother, even Anna—but no one came.

Except for him. Their leader, the one who signed all the decrees in the capital. The doyen witchfinder. A man who could stop all of this at any time—or make it so much worse.

Marching through the town square, he'd come to see his men's progress in our village. As the tinder smoldered around me, the doyen stood back and watched, smiling and tipping his hat to me, his best impression of a gentleman. My mouth nearly dry, I spat at him, and a small glob mussed up his boot. The other men rushed to clean up the mess I made, polishing the leather on their precious leader's feet, before they spat back at me. Choking on smoke, I told the fire to dance and rise up at these men, devouring them whole, but it didn't listen. The flames blossoming waist-high around my body, I finally closed my eyes and waited for it to be over.

Yet even as the straw turned to ash, my skin wouldn't melt. Nothing about me would burn at all, not so much as one singed hair. The fire kept growing stronger and higher and hotter, and I could feel it in me, sinking deeper, mingling with my bones. The same way I absorbed the spells my mother taught me, I absorbed the fire too, like it was just another lesson to learn.

"What *is* she?" the doyen said, his eyes wide and bright, as though he was almost impressed.

When the frayed ropes that bound my hands turned to cinders, I broke free, and despite everything, I ran. Out of the village, past the crossroads, and up into the forest where the witchfinders were too afraid to follow.

"Don't worry, Odette," the doyen called into the woods, his rich voice tracking me up and down the sinuous paths. "I'm saving you for last."

For last. It's the cruelest honor of all. I'm the witch who gets to wait. The one who has to watch everyone else die first.

My head spins, and I awaken again. It's daylight, and my body's not quite as heavy as before. Sometime in the night, my fever broke. I'm not sure if that's a blessing or a curse.

Outside the window, the little girl has vanished. So have the other children, leaving behind nothing except tiny smudges on the glass. On the floor, the crow is gone as well. Maybe the little girl took him with her, or maybe he left of his own accord.

There's movement outside the bedroom, and the door is open now.

"I thought I heard you." Beatrix lingers there, holding a pot of warm oatmeal.

I roll over to the edge of the bed. "What day is it?"

"Tomorrow," she says, and I wonder what that even means.

She passes me the small breakfast, and I gobble it down, my stomach raw with hunger. As I pass the bowl back to her, I glance down at her wrists, chafed and red from where the witchfinder's knotted rope tore into her skin.

"You should be resting," I whisper, but she shakes her head.

"Not when the two of you are so ill."

A chill sinks deep into me. "*Two* of us?"

"Yes," Beatrix says, not looking at me now. "You and Anna."

She's in Samuel's room, coiled up in bed, draped in enough quilts and hand-me-down blankets to smother her. Not that it matters. She's still shivering anyhow. Her arm peeks out beneath it all, the wound wrapped up tight in thick gauze, the yellow pus weeping down her skin. Her forehead glistening with a veil of sweat, she isn't awake. I'm afraid she won't ever be awake again.

Next to her, Samuel keeps vigil, his crooked rocking chair creaking in the corner, his fists clenched in his lap as if he believes rage alone might be enough to cure her.

Beatrix has tried other methods. A mountain of poultices and ointments and tonics surround the bed, empty cups of every tea she could steep, every elixir she could distill. None of it has been enough.

"Please," I say, my voice splitting in two. "Tell me there's something else we can try."

Beatrix folds her sun-spotted hands in front of her. "There are other remedies," she says. "Things we don't keep in this village."

A twinge of hope blooms inside me. "Like what?"

"Eye of star," she says. "Tansy. Dropberry."

My breath catches. These are witches' ingredients. The type you'll only find in an apothecary, stowed away like an ancient secret in far-flung alleys in far-off places.

Samuel bolts from his chair. "Tell me where they are. I'll go anywhere."

Beatrix hesitates, and her next words punch me in the gut.

"The capital," she says. "You can find them in the capital."

My head feels suddenly fevered again. Of course. That's the nearest place, the only one we could reach in time to help Anna. That city that's done this to us, where they're always at the ready with another pyre and another decree marking us for burning.

Samuel doesn't care about any of that. With Anna murmuring in her sleep, he gathers up his coat, knots his boots a little tighter. "I'll leave tonight," he says. "I'll leave *right now.*"

Beatrix shakes her head. "It won't do you any good. They won't help you."

Everything in Samuel is flattened at once. "Why not?" he asks, his voice thin and scared.

"They only help those they can trust," Beatrix says, and her eyes shift to me, the truth settling heavy as a stone on my back.

Samuel still doesn't understand. He just gapes at her. "Like who?"

I bite back tears now. "Like another witch."

Like me. If we're going to bring Anna back to us, I'll have to go to the capital.

To the place where the witchfinders are waiting for me.

chapter seven

THE BEDROOM GOES ENTIRELY STILL, THE SILENCE BREACHED ONLY BY Anna's labored breath.

"Please," I whisper, backing away. "Don't ask me to do this."

I stumble into the next room, a fire still burning in the hearth, everything as we left it even though nothing feels the same. This can't be real. This can't be the only way to bring Anna back to us.

Samuel emerges from the bedroom behind me, grumbling to himself, and he cuts a jagged path out of the house, the front door slamming in his wake. He doesn't say a word, but I can already guess where he's headed. To the stable to round up his fastest horses. On foot, we'd never make it to the capital in time.

The afternoon light pours in through the window, warming my face, and though there's no one else in the room, I'm still not alone. Outside, the little girl is waiting for me, her breath like thick clouds mushrooming against the glass.

"I can help you, Odette," she says, her voice sweet as marzipan. "I can help Anna."

She pushes nearer, the window fogging gray between us, the whole house shivering in refrain. She wants to come in, but she can't, not unless I clear away the salt circle. I'm starting to understand it now, how she and the other children are the same as the shadows.

"Please?" she asks, and a pair of dark wings flutters against the glass. The crow. *My* crow. Maybe the little girl really can help. Part of me wants to believe her, that if only I let her in, things would be different.

But before I can reach out or say another word, there's a soft shuffle of feet, and Beatrix appears beside me, gazing out the window.

"Run along now," she says to the little girl. "We don't have time for your games today."

I gape at Beatrix. "You can *see* her?"

Beatrix shrugs, moving toward the hearth. "Sometimes," she says. "That's how all those children are. Sometimes here, sometimes not here."

Breathless, I glance back toward the window where the little girl has taken Beatrix's advice and scurried off. "Where did they come from?"

Beatrix exhales a sharp laugh. "I thought you knew."

Her hands shaky, she gathers a bag of salt and charms, scribbling down the ingredients we need on a withered piece of paper. The fire flickering nearby, she brings everything over to me, but I can't help but flinch away. We linger together for a long moment, neither of us saying a word.

"I could go," Beatrix whispers finally. "If you don't want to, I could go to the capital."

My heart seizes in my chest. "No," I say. With her body hunched and frail, I could never ask this of her. She's done more than enough for me already. Now I have to do this for her. And for Anna.

The front door creaks open, and Samuel is standing there. "I'm ready," he says as though he's the one in charge of all this. Behind him in the street, two horses pace in circles, their eyes like obsidian, their whinnying cries enough to set my skin humming.

I hesitate, gazing back toward the bedroom. Inside, Anna tosses in her sleep, the fever dazing her, drawing her deeper into its embrace. If we're going to leave, we have to do it now.

My hands shaking, I turn to Beatrix. "But the men in the capital know my face," I say. "Some of the witchfinders already know what I look like."

She smiles at me. "Hide in plain sight then."

Fool them with witchcraft, she means. Those men want to see me, but I could make it so there's no me to see. A glamour to disguise myself. That is, if I have the magic left in me to do it.

The horses rear up outside, and Samuel steadies them as Beatrix drops the list along with a small satchel, heavy with enchantment, into the palm of my hand.

"Good luck, Odette," she says and disappears back into the bedroom to tend to Anna. Beatrix won't say goodbye. It's bad luck, and she knows it.

My feet heavy as granite, I move onto the street, locking the front door behind me. A palfrey, pale and strong and stubborn, waits for me, the same one I saw in the field only a few days ago. I haven't been on horseback since I was young, but I don't have any time to regain my bearings. As I mount the saddle, a few of the children are closing in, smearing past me like inkblots, their thin fingers grazing the tangled mane of my horse. The palfrey rears up, his eyes going wild.

"It's all right," I coo into his ear, and with the reins tight in my hand, I give a slight kick to his flank, and that's all it takes. We're off, headed into an afternoon as haunted as I am.

Behind me, Samuel calls out my name and scrambles onto his horse. A better rider by a mile, he catches up in an instant.

"Don't even try to get away from me," he says, and all I can do is laugh.

"Believe me," I say, "it's not you I'm afraid of."

Together, we leave these streets behind, curtains whispering as we pass, dark eyes peering out at us. I wonder if they wish us well or not.

With our horses bolting past the crossroads, there are only a few hours of daylight left. The road turning back and forth, the divots in the dirt, each dilapidated bridge swaying beneath heavy hooves.

The world is opening up before me, our path twisting through a dozen towns, maybe more, each one looking so much like our own with their taverns and churches and town squares, charred and lonesome. I've never been this far from the village before. My mother and father were too superstitious to wander past the county line, and in spite of myself, I inherited those same fears. I could have ventured beyond the forest years ago, but I never did.

At street corners, we're greeted by quiet faces marked with heartache and by garlic wreaths on every door as though they're warding off vampires and not witchfinders. Samuel and I don't stop in any of these places even though I know we should. Even though I know what's coming. The evening is sneaking in around us, and the horses sense it first. They buck beneath us, their long manes fraying, their exposed teeth glinting in the gathering moonlight.

Samuel bears down, his face lined and looking so much older than I remember him. "Steady," he commands, but the horses rise up again, their hooves digging into the mud.

I want to keep going too, I want to ride through the night, but the shadows won't let me. They're already pushing up from beneath the dirt, licking at the heels of my boots. The palfrey bolts off the road, and I let him, guiding him along a deer run until we're far enough from the path the other travelers take. A spot where we'll hopefully be safe for the night.

I slip off the saddle and take out the satchel that Beatrix gave me. She must have expected this. That's why she sent me on my way with several handfuls of salt.

"What are you doing?" Samuel is off his horse, and we're standing together now, so close it makes my stomach whirl, his eyes on me, his coat stinking of mildew and hay. I'm desperate to run from him, but I don't have time. Not with the shadows oozing up from the earth, thick as pitch.

My hands quaking, I pour a thin ring around us, saving half the salt for the trip back. If we even make it that far.

The horses safe alongside us, Samuel is in the center of the circle with me, his eyes the color of embers. "And what if I don't want to stay inside?"

I nestle down in the dirt, my legs tucked into my chest, my coat pulled tight around my throat. "Go anywhere you like," I say. "I can't stop you."

He grunts and tests the edge of the circle with the tip of his boot. I almost wonder what would happen if he were to take that final step over. Maybe nothing. The gloom isn't interested in him after all. It only seems to want me.

A wail on the wind—and the shadows push nearer to us, the darkness desperate to embrace me like a thoughtless lover.

Samuel watches it, quiet for a long moment. "So," he says finally, his lips pursed, "what does it want from you?"

My flesh tenses on my bones. "I don't know."

He scoffs. "You just cause trouble everywhere you go, don't you?" He settles down on the ground next to me. "I never understood what Anna saw in you."

I let out a laugh, sharp as glass. "That's because you never understood a lot of things."

The horses bed down near us, whining softly, their eyes still wide and restless. They don't want to be here, but they're smart enough not to run.

Samuel shoves his hands in both pockets, his nose turning pink from cold. "She never stopped worrying about you." He winces as though even remembering me is a personal insult. "I'd catch her at the window on chilly nights, always watching the forest, murmuring to herself. Like her prayers would be enough to protect you."

"Not prayers," I say and smile. "Spells."

"What's the difference?" He grunts again and shakes his head. "You and your useless magic. You always made it so hard to keep Anna safe."

He says it as though he did such a great job at protecting her. Inviting a would-be witchfinder into their house, giving up his own daughter's room, standing by and watching as the man went after her, first with the knife in the street and then in their own home. That last moment before I finished the spell against the witchfinder, when Anna was held by the throat.

When Samuel was nowhere to be found.

"What happened to you?" I stare at him. "At the end with the witchfinder. Where were you?"

Samuel looks away, his cheeks blazing red. "I was checking on him in his room, and he overtook me. Knocked me out." He exhales a strained laugh, rubbing the corner of his jaw. "Right up to the end, he was stronger than he looked."

Not strong enough though. I cover my face with both hands and try not to remember the way the witchfinder's body coiled into itself, everything about him becoming soft and formless. Even now, from miles off, I bet the dust of him is still dancing beneath the floorboards in that house as Anna struggles to take a breath and Beatrix recites another quiet spell over her.

I wish I could be back there with them in that village I've longed to escape instead of here with a man who wouldn't mind if these shadows devoured me whole. Samuel would feed me to wolves if he thought it would do him any good.

I grit my teeth, hating him a little bit more, my hands burning with rage, with power I can't use. I need to control myself. That's the only way to help Anna. I reach carefully into my pocket, still heavy with shattered glass from the spell bottle, and I pull out the red ribbon. My fingers aching, I start tying knots, one after another, right down the line. A gnarl of them, and they steady me, so I don't look up, not when Samuel keeps watching, his glare burning into me, not when he finally falls asleep, mumbling to himself through heavy dreams, not until the sun rises and the shadows withdraw at last.

My eyes bleary, I struggle to my feet, and in the naked daylight, I realize we nearly made it to the capital last night. The skyline looms before us, so close that you can smell the smolder of the factories in the morning air, pungent as rotten onion.

Next to me, Samuel breaches the salt circle and climbs atop his horse, gripping the reins tight, his knuckles blanching. He's ready to race the rest of the way there, but I hold up one hand.

"Not yet," I say and gulp down the smog-soaked air, my eyes closed, envisioning what awaits us. Those men clad in black, smirks on their faces, hands on their belts. A clocktower strikes eight in the morning, and they march through the street in a line before dispersing into every district for their hourly rounds.

There's too many of them. Beatrix was right—if I expect to get through this city, I can't go in wearing a face they could recognize.

I open my eyes and draw up what little strength I have left. The power from last night, the fury at Samuel, rises within me and turns into something I can use, this buzz in my head as though I've drank too many glasses of honey mead. Piece by piece, a glamour settles over me, my face shifting and contorting, my hair brighter, my cheekbones rounded, the flesh at the edge of my jaw tightened.

When I'm finished, I don't ask Samuel if I look different. The twist of his mouth, grimacing and hateful at the sight of my magic, is enough to tell me it's a job well done.

"I liked you better before," says a tiny voice.

The little girl. She's sitting on the back of Samuel's horse, looking like she belongs there. She must have followed us in the night. She probably *is* the night, part of the darkness doing its best to track me down wherever I go.

"Leave me alone," I whisper, but even as I climb atop my saddle, she just grins, hitchhiking on the back of the horse unbeknown to Samuel, the fool he is. I try to outrun her, but Samuel keeps up with me, close enough that the little girl is only inches away, still giving me that same gap-toothed grin.

"Your skin doesn't scorch through your clothes," she says and nods at my jacket, draped over me like a shroud. "It doesn't hurt the horses either."

"No," I say, my hands steady against the palfrey's back. "I can only burn another person."

The wind whips bitterly around us, and the little girl tilts her head at me. "But why?"

"I don't know," I say. "Maybe because people are the ones who lit the flames, so they're the only ones who can feel them."

Samuel scoffs as the gates to the capital come into view. "Speaking with ghosts again?" he asks.

I flash him a half-smile. "Better than speaking with you," I say, and we ride together across a rickety bridge and into this bustling, hideous city.

Along the slender streets, we dismount from our horses and lead them behind us. There are people all around, selling bread and trinkets and promises, their eyes hungry, their faces gaunt. I keep my shoulders folded into me, careful not to touch anyone or anything. A sheen of decay hangs over this city like a stained bridal veil, everything around us towering and oppressive. This place is a fortress and a prison all wrapped up in beveled stone. It's almost beautiful in its own way—or would be if the witchfinders weren't everywhere. Those boots, those cloaks, those dark gazes that are always watching and waiting for you to reveal yourself.

Still on their hourly rounds, they march right past us, and I freeze, holding my breath, trying not to let even the slightest movement of my body disturb the air around me. If I'm quiet enough, if I pretend I don't exist at all, maybe they won't notice me.

Samuel, on the other hand, isn't eager to wait. Though he stops to let the men pass, he fidgets the whole time, his hand on his horse's flank, fingernails nearly digging into the animal's flesh. This is all an inconvenience to him, waiting on the witchfinders to go by. He's never learned to be afraid the way I have.

The crowd parts down the middle, and a group of men lead a girl in shackles past us, their latest conquest. Her face is down, her cheeks are flushed. She's young, almost younger than I was when I cast my first spell. A child really.

I drift forward, sparks of weak magic flickering within me. These men terrify me, but after everything that's happened over these past few days, it terrifies me more to do nothing. I want to help this girl, the way no one ever helped me. Whatever I could do for her probably isn't enough. I'm probably too exhausted to make a difference, but I need to try.

I start to move toward them just as Samuel steps in front of me, blocking the way.

"Steady," he commands as though I'm another wild animal to tame, and before I can even argue with him, the witchfinders have already vanished around a corner, spiriting their prisoner to a fate I know all too well. I'm too late, the same as always.

"Why are the men doing this?" the little girl whispers, and I shake my head.

Maybe it's for the glory. Maybe it's because they honestly believe they're keeping the peace. Maybe it's simply for something to do, a way to earn a living.

That's just it though—it doesn't matter why. Any reason they have will never be enough. It won't take away the pain, and it won't make them stop.

With the men gone for now, Samuel ties up his horse with a haphazard loop and shoves a path right through the marketplace. Into the heart of this city and away from me.

"Wait," I call after him and tether the palfrey to a stone post, double knotting his reins.

His hands bundled into fists, Samuel forges on, searching the signs overhead, cursing all the while. He thinks he'll discover the apothecary by running fast enough, but that's not how it works. Places like this are always easy to miss, especially if you're looking for them. As he pushes through the crowd, the merchants back away from him, murmuring to themselves, their gazes sliding past us like prying fingers. The people notice him. They notice *us*. He's going to ruin this. Samuel and I are outsiders in this city. That means we're not to be trusted.

I catch up with him, nearly breathless now. "You'll never find it this way."

Samuel sneers, his chapped lips peeling back from his teeth. "And how would you do it?"

"Like a witch," I say and cut a circuitous path in front of him, around wooden barrels of freshly caught carp, their stench simmering in the sun. Pressed against the stone buildings, my fingertips pass along the mortar, looking for a sign, a weakness, somewhere that's a little different.

With Samuel and the little girl lagging behind me, I push around a corner and down a thin alley that reeks of vervain and secrets. To a door so narrow it looks more like a shadow. I start toward it, but I glance back at Samuel first. He's standing there, gaping at me.

I watch him, the truth lodging in my throat. "You can't see it," I say.

That's how they keep the witchfinders from discovering them. That's how there are any witches left here.

"I won't be long," I say and turn toward the stone. "You'll have to wait."

Samuel charges forward, his whole body quivering. "I didn't come this far—"

My head snaps back toward him. "Do you want Anna to die?"

The question instantly deflates him. He falls back a few steps, his shoulders sagging, and I won't wait for him to argue again.

"I'll keep an eye on him," the little girl says brightly as I move toward the wall and disappear into it.

Inside, the place opens up into serpentine corridors, dust bathing everything, the light so dim at first I can barely see my own hands in front of my face. There are rooms tucked inside rooms, candles puddling wax on the floor. Every corner smells of burning myrrh and rosemary culled fresh from the stem. It's smoky and strange, and it almost feels like home. I only wish it was.

There are other witches everywhere, curled up and mumbling in corners, still casting spells even while they're asleep. There are cliques of them too, seated cross-legged in salt circles and stone circles and circles only they can see. They eye me up as I pass, a stranger in their midst, but I look away and keep walking. Through curtains slung over doorways and spiderwebs as dainty as bobbin lace.

In the furthest room, away from all the rest, a woman waits behind a counter. There are dozens of shelves around her, bottles stacked upon bottles, hundreds of herbs and stones, almost any component a witch could ever need.

The woman watches me, and I nod back at her. "Hello," I say, but she says nothing in return.

Maybe this is how it's done. Quietly and carefully. After all, the best way not to get caught is to not make a fuss. I slip the piece of paper across the counter, the list of ingredients inscribed in Beatrix's meticulous cursive. Then I wait, my hands folded in front of me.

The woman looks straight through me, unblinking, never bothering to glance at the paper. "There's nothing we can do for you," she says.

My heart stills in my chest. "That's not true." I push the list closer to her. "It's only a few items."

She'll die without your help, I nearly scream, but this woman probably already knows that, and she's still shaking her head anyhow.

"I'm sorry," she says, but she doesn't mean it. If she were really sorry, she would do something. This last-ditch effort to cure Anna, so close to me now yet just as far away as it was when I was back in the village. I'm not welcome out there with the people in the capital, but somehow, I'm not welcome in here with my own kind either.

I want to say something else—I want to reason with her—but a pair of figures appear at my side, their shadows nearly choking the life out of me. I'm not sure if they're men or monsters, but what I do know is they're going to shove me out of this place, back onto the street, and then all of this will be for nothing.

"Please don't," I say as they put their hands on me and immediately regret it.

It's a burst of smoke and wails and then a silence saturating the room thicker than glue.

I back away into the corner, folding my arms over me. Everyone's here and watching me now. This room isn't very big, but from the hallway, they all manage to jumble together, dozens of them, to get a view of me. The witches from the other rooms, their circles and their spells broken. They heard the commotion, and now they want to see me. This thing that caused it. They move closer, people stuffed into every crevice, this place where they hide away from the world. The one safe haven left. All the witches in the city must be here.

This catches in my throat. *All of them.* Including one I know too.

She pushes into the room, later than the rest, maybe the very last witch in the capital to get a glimpse of me.

"Hello, sister," she says, that same crooked smile on her face.

"Hello, Freya."

The woman behind the counter gapes at us. "*You* brought her here?" she asks my sister.

Freya chirps up a laugh. "Odette brought herself," she says. "I never could tell her where to go."

This hurts more than it should, the memory of us at the crossroads the last time we saw each other. My throat tightening, I turn back toward the woman and nudge the list farther across the counter.

"Please," I say. "This is all I need. Then I'll be gone. I promise."

The woman picks up the thin paper, her fingers gentle and cautious as though she's selecting a sweet biscuit for high tea.

"I'll see what I can do," she says and disappears behind a row of wooden shelves.

All around me, the other witches are still watching, though none of them speak or move toward me. I wonder if they've heard of me before, if the witchfinders' stories have gotten to them too. And if so, I wonder what they think of me. If they hate me for not dying, the same way I hate myself.

I look away and run my hands through my hair, these golden locks that aren't mine. I'd forgotten that I'm not me right now. The glamour is holding strong, this face that only I should be able to see through. One that Freya can see through too. I never could fool her.

She watches me, still smiling. "What are you doing here?"

I shake my head. "It's nothing," I say, and she tosses back her head and lets out a cackle.

"Oh, it's a lot more than that. You wouldn't come for nothing."

I draw in a sharp breath. Again, I never could fool her.

"It's for Anna," I say. "She's been hurt."

Freya hesitates. "A witchfinder?" she asks, and I nod. "Is he still in the village?"

"No," I say, and instantly, my sister's face brightens.

"So I didn't dream it after all." She leans in, her eyes glinting gold. "You turned his guts to porridge, didn't you? Left him for dust?"

The other witches are all inspecting me closer now, curious how I did it, how I did in a witchfinder. My stomach corkscrews, and I fumble with my hands, with air.

"It was one time," I say, "and it nearly killed me."

Freya beams at me, but I turn away as the woman returns from behind the shelves. Her brow twisted, she slides a small bottle toward me, the cork sealed in red wax. This is it, what I came for. I drop my last coin on the counter along with the charms Beatrix placed in the satchel. It's a modest gift—a few buttons, a golden clasp, a chip of amethyst—but it must be enough because the woman scoops everything into her hand, and for the first time, she smiles at me.

"Thank you," she says, and I imagine it's been a long time since any stranger in this city offered something to a witch rather than took it away.

Grasping the tiny bottle in my hand, I dart for the hallway, the way I came, the other witches falling back to make room for me. Everyone's glad I'm leaving now. Everyone except one person.

"Odette, wait." Freya is following behind me. "You don't need to run this time."

"That's funny," I say, "coming from you."

"It's different now," she says. "We can be safe here."

"No, we can't." I whirl around to face her. "They already know who I am, Freya. Or didn't you hear what happened to me after you left?"

Her eyes go dark now. "I'm sorry," she whispers, and something in her face shifts.

I know this look. It's the same one she used to get when we were children, back when she was caught. She wants to tell me everything—how she shouldn't have left me behind, alone in the village, perfect fodder for those men. And she's got to recognize this look on me too, how I know I shouldn't have been foolish enough to stay, that I should have run with her when I still had the chance. We should have stuck together.

But neither of us say those things. I tuck the bottle of herbs into the lining of my jacket, a place where the witchfinders might not think to look. Without a word, I slip through the stone and back out the door.

On the other side, Samuel is still loitering in the alley.

"What took you so long?" he asks, and overhead, the sun is high and unrelenting, shimmering off all the stone buildings, so bright it's blinding. I must have been in there for hours even though it only felt like a few minutes.

"I thought you weren't coming back," Samuel says, and I scoff at him. As though I'd abandon Anna now.

On the street, I make my way through the crowd, narrowing my shoulders. The clocktower strikes three in the afternoon, and I turn back once. Samuel and the little girl are behind me, but my sister hasn't followed us. Of course, she didn't. She and I have made our choices, and they don't include each other.

We're back to our horses, tied up and waiting for us, and I start to climb atop the palfrey, so close to making that last sprint out of the city gates and back toward the village. A sharp murmur cuts through the crowd, and all I hear for a long, devastating moment is the melody of those footsteps. A gait as steady as spring rain, unforgiving as a maelstrom.

The crowd splits in two, and for a bottomless instant, no one speaks, no one moves, and I know why. The sun shifts overhead, and here he is, moving among us, more phantom than man.

The doyen witchfinder.

Towering above everyone, he drifts through the crowd, smiling and nodding as though he truly wants us to believe he's one of us. An ordinary man on an ordinary day and not the flesh and blood that nightmares are made of.

The others on the street stand still, waiting for this to be over. This inspection of his, always looking for another name to jot down in his ledger.

I inhale sharply as he steps toward me, his eyes shrouded beneath the wide brim of his cavalier hat. I can barely see him, but I see more than enough. Everything in my body is ready to split at the seams, but I won't let myself fall apart now. Magic buzzing in my bones, the spell holds steady, and he passes me by without so much as a second glance.

Nearby, our horses shift and snort, and Samuel glances at me, his face wan but determined. It's almost time. We're almost safe again.

But there's someone else here too. Someone pursuing a witchfinder and not the other way around.

"Sir, please listen to me."

This is a voice I recognize. My gaze flicks up, searching the crowd. A merchant in the street dodges this way, and a fishmonger's wife moves that way, and all at once, she materializes in front of me. The face from the witchfinder's locket. The sister of the man I murdered.

I try to keep myself stitched together, to keep the energy in me steady, but she wanders closer, and I feel it within me, my magic slipping, the veil of my glamour about to tear in two.

"Sir, just tell me. Have you seen him?" she says, stumbling through the street, desperate to get the witchfinder's attention. "Do you know where he's gone?"

She's moving toward me now, so near that I can feel it in her. That grief as potent as mine. She knows loss so intimately, all thanks to me.

I start to turn away, ready to mount my horse and gallop back to the village, never stopping, never looking back again, but she sees me first. Her lips mouth a silent prayer, and beyond reason, she recognizes my face too.

"You," she whispers, and with a trembling hand, she reaches out for me.

It only takes an instant, but it feels like so much longer, the images slowing in my mind.

Her hand on my arm.

The scorching of her palm against my skin.

That stench of burning flesh wafting up like rot on an August afternoon.

A mournful scream that quivers through her and down into the earth, shaking me to my marrow.

My mouth droops open, ready to scream too or to comfort her or quiet her, but it's already too late. The doyen is lingering at the edge of the crowd, almost gone from here, but as this girl cradles her seared hand, wailing to the sky, he turns back, and instantly, I'm caught.

He cuts back through the crowd like a knife. I try to slip away and run, but the faces are clotting all around me. Their eyes curious, and their hands grasping but too afraid to touch because they know what I am. This urban legend they've heard about. A witch who wouldn't burn. I'm a curiosity to them, a dubious salvation. They'd rip me to pieces and sell off pounds of my flesh if they thought it might save them. If they really believed it would stop the witchfinders from burning them too.

But nothing will stop these men, especially not their leader. The doyen pushes past the others, his steps quickening, until he's standing right in front of me, his breath thick with spiced tobacco and fatty meat buttered up and falling off the bone. Everything about him is too much, too rich, precisely the way he demands it.

I want to stand tall against him, holding myself together, holding this veil over me, but next to me, the girl from the locket cries out again.

"He's gone, isn't he?" she asks, her voice shattering. "My brother's dead."

This agony in her, this pain that I've caused. It shatters me too, and all my resolve is lost in an instant. The glamour dissolves around me, and my face returns. The same face he recognizes.

Smiling like a proper gentleman, the doyen tips his hat and bows to me.

"Good morning, Odette," he says, and the whole world falls apart.

chapter eight

Backed against the stone wall, I can't run from him. He'll catch me no matter which way I turn. Besides, the crowd is still pushing closer at the edges, their faces lined and gray, the color of faded pewter. There's no chance I could cut through all of them and make it to the other side, all the way to the road that leads out of the capital.

I'm trapped in this city I never wanted to see with a man I've seen too well. Everything about him is the same as I remember it, luxurious and cruel as though life is merely a passing diversion to him. He certainly makes sure that's what it is for others. So fleeting they might blink and miss their own existence, burned to cinders on his command.

Samuel and the little girl stand among the scared faces, frozen there in this bustling marketplace, only a few yards from me and a universe away too.

I wish they'd run. They could still get back to the village by nightfall, just the two of them. They don't need to stay and watch me die, and they certainly don't need to risk dying themselves.

I look to them, sharpening my mind, my thoughts, trying to speak or scream without ever making a sound, but the doyen draws nearer to me, his cloak billowing, enveloping us in an almost-embrace.

"So," he says, rolling the word off his tongue like he's savoring a fine wine, "what brings you to my city?"

I tip up my chin and steel myself to him. "Not you," I say.

His smile never fading, he runs one steady hand through a wisp of my hair, his fingertips smoldering, his gaze all over me as though I already belong to him.

Near us, the girl from the locket has collapsed into herself, weeping, her body in a heap. The doyen glances at her as though she's a gadfly, invading his picnic, before he turns back to me.

"So you're the one who took care of her brother, that hopeful little witchfinder?" he asks. "We wondered where he went. The men missed having their boots shined."

He rasps out a laugh that sets my flesh crawling. For the first time, I imagine the man I murdered as he must have been among these privileged few in the capital. A grunt, a joke, a figure as insubstantial as mist to them. Although he hadn't figured it out yet, he never would have been one of them. They couldn't have allowed that.

That's how he ended up the way he was, angry at being invisible, looking for someone to blame. Their boots in his back, his hand on Anna's throat. This cycle that never ends.

The horses rear up, and the little girl inches forward, her back arched. She wants to help, maybe Samuel does too if only because the waxed bottle from the apothecary is still inside my jacket. I exhale to call them off, to scream at them to run, but no sound comes out as the doyen leans in a little closer, nearly smothering the life from my body.

"I'm so glad he didn't get to you first," he whispers, his lips pressed almost to my ear. "I meant it when I said I was saving you for last."

For last. A day that's finally come. A loop of frayed rope hangs from his belt, and his fingers twitch toward it, ready to bind me up. Maybe he'll try fire again, or maybe he'll be more creative this round. After all, there are so many methods to murder a girl, and he has ample time now to perfect his technique.

I choke up a sob and try to turn away from him. There, still curled up on the street, the sister of the witchfinder gazes back at me, her eyes webbed with red, her throat ragged from sorrow. This moment of grief passes between us, and as if by an invisible hand, the locket slips out of my jacket and lands with a gentle thud on the street. It snaps opens, and she looks down, suddenly staring at her own face. This picture, this final relic of her brother, proof that he carried her with him everywhere he went, even when he went places he shouldn't have.

Her face twists, and I can feel it. Something is rising up from deep within her, a fury more dangerous than the witchfinder's decree. She exhales another wail, but it's different this time. The melody is like fingernails scraping across a coffin lid and the bubbling of something in a cast-iron pot finally burning over. My bones feel liquid beneath my skin, and the rage inside her spirals out, materializing in a sharp crescendo like a thunderclap of the gods. The weight of it forces me and this man apart as if she wants to be the one to finish me.

The doyen stumbles backward, nearly crashing into the crowd, and this is it, my only chance. I gulp down air and surge forward. The swarming faces haven't stopped gaping at me, their gaunt hands outstretched and still wanting my body, my power. But they know it isn't safe to touch me, and this is all I need, an instant of their hesitation, enough time for me to slice through the throng and make it to the other side.

I glance back once. The doyen is already shoving through the crowd, spitting and cursing and pushing past the witchfinder's sister as she scrambles in the dirt to pick up the necklace, the only heirloom left of her brother. She doesn't seem to know what she did, all the power she holds inside. It must have been an accident, one that saved my life.

The worn soles of my boots slip between the crevices in the street, the bottle of herbs heavy in my jacket. I'm running the wrong direction, away from the gates of the capital and back toward the apothecary. It's the only path that's clear, but that doesn't mean it's a way out. Down the alley, the door to where the witches are hiding has already vanished. They're smart enough to know when to turn their back on the world. I don't blame them, but I certainly envy them for it, how they keep themselves safe.

"Odette." The doyen's voice wafts after me, tracking me around every corner and along each new street. I stumble forward, running for a moment before stopping to catch a breath that never comes. My hands numb, I'm still hollowed out from all this magic, and I'm not convinced I can cobble myself back together long enough to outrun him.

The streets are narrow, stone walls and towering buildings on every side, and it's like racing through a catacomb. At last, I come to a clearing between the buildings, overwhelmed with the sound of something rushing past. Squinting in the bare sun, I shield my eyes and try to make sense of this place. It's a kind of derelict market, arrayed with spindly docks and lonely fishmongers whose wrinkled faces have seen more than they care to tell. Old splintered boats have been pulled to shore, stacked up in makeshift piles, and it doesn't look like this place has been used for what it's good for in years.

That's because of who lives here now. I gaze across a thin bridge, and everything in my chest constricts.

This is the Wharf District. I'm right in the heart of where the witchfinders dwell.

I cling to the stone railing near a bridge, my head spun, the river whispering below me as if alive. What a cruel irony that these men light a thousand flames, yet they've settled by the water. Maybe they believe that's the only way the fires won't follow them home.

Unknown faces drift past me. Some of them are merchants, their eyes vacant, fearful as I am. Others are the very men who terrorize us, dressed in their boots and cloaks, wearing those dubious grins that never seem to fade. They look right at me, but they just keep passing by. The land's deluged with witchfinders, a hundred or more of them scattered throughout the city and on commission to far-flung villages. There are so many in fact that none of these particular men know me by sight. Not yet anyhow. Their leader will fix that soon enough. He'll catch up to me if I don't keep moving. But the only way out is through, right past the homes where these men rest their wicked bones every night.

I breathe deep and think of Anna. It's not much farther back to her now. Just across this water and past a few houses, and I'll be on the other side, that much closer to freedom. From there, I can circle back around to the city gates. I remember these roads from the maps that Freya used to hide from our mother. If I'm careful, I can find my way out.

My head down, I start across the bridge, but something in the air knocks me back a step. I cover my face with both hands, the stench overwhelming, that sickly sweet perfume of rot and melancholy. It's unmistakable. There's death all around me, but I don't know where it's coming from, and no one else seems concerned about it. The merchants move back and forth, mumbling to themselves as though this is an ordinary day.

I need to pretend it's all ordinary too. I need to keep moving. Another step across the bridge, but the reek hits me again, stronger this time, so close it must be right here, right next to me.

Or right beneath me. My guts twisting, I peer over the stone railing, and the whole world stops.

Below, in the water, there are bodies stacked upon bodies, hands and feet bound in half-disintegrated rope. Dozens of girls deposited in the brackish brine along with yesterday's garbage. Girls with families, with names, with voices that the witchfinders plucked from their throats with a nothing flick of a wrist.

Some of them are bobbing there just beneath the waves, others weighted down and heavy with bloat, their jaws broken so that their mouths are always gaping open now in a wail that will never end. A few of them haven't withered at all, their faces rosy, their arms crossed neatly over their chests. All their eyes are closed as though they're merely dreaming there in the river, waiting for someone to wake them up again.

I know what this means. They're swimming witches, dropping them like stones into the water and waiting to see if they float. If the accused bobs back to the surface, the men claim it means the water has rejected them, that they're impure, that they're deserving of execution. And if they don't come back up, *Well then,* the men would say, *that's just a pity, isn't it?*

Bile rises up my throat, and I want to scream. I want to plunge my hands into this filthy river and yank out each body one by one and do my best to breathe life back into them. Not that it will do any good. They're long gone, and I can't help them now. I should keep moving, but part of me can't just walk away.

So I keep staring as though that will be enough to stop the world from forgetting them. There are so many, clogging up the currents of the river. Somewhere, undoubtedly, a cistern is backing up with rot, gagging and poisoning whole families, but these witchfinders don't care so long as their own water and wine come from elsewhere. Why should they be bothered to worry about the ones they'll murder tomorrow? After all, this river is a message, a perpetual reminder of the divide between these men and the rest of us, of what will happen if you dare cross them.

And they're not done yet, not by a long shot. On the other side of the bridge, the witchfinders are gathering, ready to add another to the river, her hands bound, her face soft and defeated.

I recognize this girl from earlier, the one they marched down the street past us. She's young, frail as chipped porcelain. That doesn't mean a thing to these men. A witch is a witch no matter her age. Better to get her early before she has a chance to do her worst.

The girl is quiet while they tighten the ropes around her. Her hair, clumped and oily, hangs across her face like she's shielding her eyes to keep from seeing what happens next. Her arms and face are covered in red wheals, and I recognize the wounds at once—from the witchfinders' needles. These men must have poked and prodded her for hours, maybe even days, testing every mole and freckle on her body. That's how they say they can discover if you're a witch: puncture the mark, and if you don't bleed, it's incontrovertible proof of your wickedness.

This is a lie of course. I have no such spot anywhere on me, and nobody would dare claim I'm not a witch. Their pricking proves nothing, and it means nothing, but the witchfinders don't care how flimsy the evidence is so long as they have something to write down in their ledger. A so-called reason why they turned you to ash.

The men draw closer to her, those hideous smiles on their faces, as they prepare to lift her up on the count of three. When they're finished, they'll leave her body in the water with the rest. They've probably run out of room in the earth long ago. There aren't enough cemeteries in this city to accommodate what they've done.

The sun is well past its precipice now, and the men secure their grasp on her slight body.

"One," they say in unison.

No one moves forward to help her. The people are allowed to watch, but they aren't allowed to object or to weep. There's no mourning at the executions. The witchfinders have outlawed it. If you want to cry, you have to do that in your home behind lock and key. Otherwise, these men will accuse you of sympathizing with witches, of being a witch, and then you'll find yourself bobbing in the bottom of the river too.

That means everyone—the fishmongers, the merchants, the tourists, the widows—just has to stand and watch as those clumsy, cruel hands paw at her body. A final insult before they finish her. The witchfinders grin and guffaw, their fingers everywhere at once, but the girl doesn't cry or move or utter a word. If anything, she's probably been expecting this for months, preparing herself night after night for this inevitable moment as though this is only a rite of passage and not a death knell.

"Two," they say, their bodies quivering with glee.

All around me, the people start slipping past, headed away from this spectacle. They already know how this will end. I could keep going too. No one is watching me, the witchfinders far too preoccupied with the day's execution. In this moment, I'm nothing and nobody, an invisible cipher who can slide right through. I could circle around this district and make my way toward the road that leads out of the city. That one path that will take me back to the village, back to Anna, back to the closest thing I can call safety.

But then there's this girl. Another moment will tick by on the clocktower, and she'll be in the water, drowning for no good reason. I fumble in my pocket for the satchel that Beatrix gave me. There's a single handful of salt left. It was supposed to be for my return trip to the village in case I'm stranded in the dark overnight again. It could be good for something else too.

I'm already shaky on my feet. After the glamour, after everything, I don't know if I have enough left in me to do this.

But I have to try.

"Three." They're lifting her, they're ready, but so am I, the salt falling between my fingers like sand in an hourglass. It's a hasty circle, but it's enough. My head lolls back, and I draw up the fire these men put inside me. I let it flow within my body, and then I focus it away from me, out of me, and into somewhere else. Below, the water goes calm, its surface slick as ice, and a thin border of flames surround me, rising from the ring of salt.

Nearby, the fishmongers murmur and back away from me, but they don't stop watching. The other merchants and the widows and the passersby stop and stare as well. For the first time, someone in this capital is putting on a better show than the witchfinders.

And with the fire twitching higher around me, the witchfinders finally notice too. Shouts ricochet between them, confusion and ire rising and falling like restless waves, and they hastily divide themselves in two, half of them staying with the girl and the other half starting toward me. I don't have much time before they knot their ropes around my body and deposit me in the water like week-old chum.

Fortunately, I don't need much time. From within me, I draw up the fire and focus it toward this girl, giving her my power, giving her a way out. I've never done this before, so I can't even be sure that it will work. But with all the men watching me, I watch her, and the magic takes hold, the ropes that bind her contorting and writhing and shriveling to black.

At first, she doesn't know she's free. Everyone's so used to being afraid of these men that she doesn't even think there could be another way.

"Run," I mouth to her, and she gazes down at her hands as the ropes fall away into ash. The sun in her eyes, she seizes up for an agonizing moment, her face twisted as if she's measuring the distance to the nearest shadow or alley or corner. As if it might not be worth her trying to escape at all. Now that they've had her, they'll never stop looking for her. I can attest to that much.

But then something in her eyes flashes gold, and she takes a single step forward. Next to her, one of the men realizes she's broken free, and his hands are on her, tightening around her wrists. Exhaling a guttural moan, she rips herself away and scratches at his cheeks, his eyes, his throat, baring her teeth at him, baring everything left in her. He lifts one arm to strike her across the mouth, hard enough that it might knock her out cold, but she's faster than he is. With a pivot as graceful as a dancer's, she turns and leaps, gliding off into the afternoon, her body lithe and strong and all her own. Stunned, the witchfinders gape at her, a few of them starting after her, the others still coming after me.

I wilt backward, the rest of the magic emptying out of me, spiriting the girl on her way. One last flash around a building, and she's gone, outrunning the men at least for now.

But on the stone ground, I can't outrun anyone. The witchfinders are marching straight for me, their faces pale and melding into one, and I curl into myself, my knees skinned, my hands gnarled, all the enchantment unspooling from me like a tangled bolt of yarn.

Dizzy, I part my lips to weep, but something else comes out. A long whistle, sweet and sharp, one I almost don't recognize anymore. It's the bird call that Anna and I used as children.

The men have reached me now, their shadows stretching over my body. Their knives unsheathed, these men blot out the sun, and I turn away, nothing in me eager to witness my own end.

Then I hear it—the gentle patter of a thousand wings. The men hesitate, their faces scrunched up and glowering. They turn toward the sky, but they're looking the wrong way.

I inhale a heavy breath, and all at once, the crows and cardinals and collared doves break through the reflective surface of the river as though they're shattering a looking glass. All these ghosts tangle around us in an instant, their weightless feathers sloughing off water like droplets of blood.

There's a cacophony of screams and sobs as the men flail uselessly at the air, swatting right through the birds who can't be bothered by the touch of a witchfinder.

There are other birds joining in too. The starlings sneak up through the water, fashionably late to the gathering, their beaks pecking at the writhing men. Goldfinches and blackbirds and house sparrows too, materializing in the river among the dead and rising to join us. They're at once here and not here, thin as smoke, thick as thieves. Their voices are still silent in their throats, but they won't let that stop them.

Nearby, the fishmongers take cover as the witchfinders stumble and shriek and thrash their arms as though attempting to fly away themselves. A few collapse to the ground and start clawing at me, their hands calloused, their fingernails raking across my flesh. It burns them to touch me, but right now with these phantom birds snarled in their cloaks, they don't care. They just want me to stop, they want everything to stop.

And so do I. All I want is to be out of this place. Crawling on hands and knees, I make it halfway across the bridge before one of the men gets close enough to pin me down with his boot. I struggle beneath him, the flames in me burning through the sole of the leather, but he doesn't notice. Instead, he removes a knife from his belt and raises it above his head, ready to bury it in what's left of my heart. But he's not nearly fast enough. A crow—my crow, the one that won't stay buried—twists and turns in the air, thrashing against his own broken wings before diving right at the man. A quick snip-snap of that split beak, and a red line appears across the witchfinder's cheek. The gash is as fine as a paper cut but bleeding all the same, a stream of crimson coming stronger now like thick tears, and the man wails, swatting at my crow who's already soared into the sky, preparing to dive again.

Revenge simmering in my heart, I limp away from the fray, and I'm almost across the bridge when a voice more ferocious than the rest rises up to greet me.

"Look at all this lovely chaos."

The doyen witchfinder. He's standing in the middle of the bridge, which means I can't go back the way I came, and with the witchfinders hollering and flailing in the Wharf District, I can't go that way either. I'm trapped between—the same place I'm always caught.

The doyen drifts toward me, and I brace against the stone, struggling to my feet, but with everything heavy inside me, I'm not quick enough. He reaches out toward me, and I'm convinced he's ready to smother me or strangle me or shove me into the water. He does something worse. His fingers nimble and unforgiving, he tears at my jacket and yanks the bottle of Anna's herbs from inside the lining, the place I hid it because I honestly believed none of them would ever look there.

"I need that," I whisper, gritting my teeth.

He cradles it to his chest. "So do I."

I grimace because I know why. He wants it as evidence of my crimes—and evidence of others' crimes in this city. No doubt he's been searching for the apothecary in the Market District for months. Now thanks to me, he's one step closer to discovering them.

Above us, the birds are fading into the air, their bodies turning translucent as water. Beautiful but voiceless, these ghosts aren't strong enough to do their worst. That's because I'm not strong enough. If only I could make them real and whole again, if only I could give them back their melodies and let them sing so loud that these men would scream and clutch their bleeding ears. But right now, I can barely stand.

The doyen scoffs as the rest of the birds vanish. "Nice trick, Odette. Have you got another?"

He forces the bottle into his pocket, and with one last glint of a smile, he's gone, vanished across the bridge and back into the crowd toward the Wharf District. He took the one thing I can't live without, that Anna can't live without. I didn't come all this way to turn around and go home with nothing. I won't let Anna die because of these men.

I drag myself along, doing my best to run, keeping in step with him, not letting the doyen out of my sight. Across the bridge, around the witchfinders who reach out for me but can't quite take hold, the birds still dizzying their heads. Their fingertips brush against me, bits of smoke rising from their skin where they touch me. I wrench away, whipping around a sharp corner, and there he is, the doyen slipping down an alley and disappearing through the side door of a house.

I hesitate, not wanting to follow, not wanting to walk inside and find out what's waiting there. But with the others hollering at my back, finally staggering to their feet, this is the only place I can go that they might not see me. I hold my breath and dart through the door.

Inside, it's all vaulted ceilings and winding staircases and gold cornices. There's no decay on anything, the whole world wiped clean, everything so dazzling it makes your eyes ache. A place that's far too opulent just like the witchfinders, demanding your attention and reminding you of all that you'll never have.

A sharp laugh in a far-off room, and I follow the sound, edging down a wide hallway, past portraits glowering at me. Generations of men, coiffed and tailored, grins on their faces and bureaucracy in their hearts. In a tucked-away room, a fire flickers up beneath a mantle, and I see my own face staring back at me in a burnished mirror on the wall. It's disorienting in here, the walls black, the light otherwise dim, and it takes me a moment to realize what room this is.

A parlor, *his* parlor.

He waits in the corner, watching me. I want to run, but I can't turn back, not yet. Between us, there's a long table with a pressed scarlet sash draped over it and an oil lamp unlit in the center. Two silver plates are set up at either end, one smeared with grease and arrayed with lemon rinds and pomegranate seeds and chicken bones gnawed down to the marrow, the other untouched, beef fat congealing and puddling around boiled potatoes.

The doyen smiles. "You can have her leftovers if you'd like," he says and nods at the immaculate plate. "I doubt she's coming back for them."

I seize up in the doorway. This was for the girl I set free, her final supper. He brings the accused here first before they're bound and gagged and walked to the water or the pyre or the gallows. He wines and dines them before he executes them.

That's why he led me to his home. This is another trap, and one I waltzed right into.

"I hoped I'd have a chance to show you around." With the flourish of one hand, he motions to the end of the table. "Sit. Please."

I lace my fingers together in front of me to keep from shaking. "No, thank you," I say.

Outside, shouts echo off the brickwork as the others surround the house. I can't get away now, not that I would even try, not without that bottle from the apothecary.

The doyen knows this. He drifts around the empty chairs, practically weightless, his footsteps not making a sound as though he's not flesh and blood at all but merely a ghost floating.

I stumble away from him and along the wall, closer to the window, but I'm not quick enough. With a strong hand, he lifts one of the chairs and shoves it at me, a leg striking me square in my chest and forcing me onto my back on the table. Behind me, the unlit lamp tumbles over, spewing yellow streams of oil down the table sash and dripping onto the floor.

"I told you to sit," he says. He's leaning over me now, one hand on either side of me, his body as close as he can get without touching me, that warm breath snaking down my throat and stealing the air from my lungs, the same way the witchfinders steal everything else.

This is meant to unravel me, but it also does me a favor. He's close to me, and so is what he stole. I force one hand into his pocket. He clasps my wrist for a moment, his eyes going black, but the pain sears through him, and with a sharp howl, he lets me go just as I rip the bottle from his jacket. Then I break away from beneath him, stumbling from the table and backing toward the hall.

I make it to the doorway, sliding Anna's cure back into my jacket lining, but a thunder of footsteps moves closer. The side door where I came in opens, and I glance in the mirror suspended over the mantle, their reflections shimmering there. They're here now, all the witchfinders, dozens of them, pouring into the parlor, a long line of them snaking back around and down the hall. There isn't enough room for all of them in this house, but they're used to pushing into places where they don't belong.

They're everywhere now, and they won't let me go this time. The man who raised his knife to me in the street, the one with a thin cut of red across his cheek, moves toward me, rope in his hand, ready to bind me up, but I lunge forward and take hold of his arm. His face twists, and he exhales a banshee cry as the flames in me rise up in him. His arm and clothes are alight, and without hesitating, I yank his still burning cloak off his body and drape it over the spilled oil from the lamp. The table blooms bright orange, flames and soot rising up to the ceiling, everything clouded and heavy and hot.

The fire disorients the witchfinders—it's funny how afraid they are when the flames are licking at their bodies instead—and as they scream and curse, staggering this way and that, I collapse to my knees, clawing my way across the hardwood floor, gagging up smoke. I have to find a window, some way out, but even with my hands searching the walls, I still can't find my way, and I can't breathe.

Then there's the sound of breaking glass and a spray of diamonds around me. I look up, and there's a hand on my arm and a voice I recognize.

"Odette."

Freya. She followed me after all. Through the shattered window, she entwines her fingers with mine and pulls me out of the smoke-filled house. I'm burning right into her, but she won't let me go.

On the street, I crash to the ground, my jacket torn, my knees bleeding. Soot clogs my lungs, and even in the open air, I can barely see, the world turning swimmy and strange at the edges of my vision. Next to me, Freya rocks back and forth, clasping her peeling hands together, trying to chase away the pain of me. Another moment holding me, and she would have been ablaze the same way as that man in the parlor.

The little girl stands nearby. "I told you she was inside," she says to Freya.

"How did you find me?" I ask, wheezing.

"We heard you call out to the birds." The little girl beams at me. "From there, we just followed the men's screams."

Struggling to our feet, Freya and I make it to a narrow alley between a row of houses, the witchfinders calling out behind us. I get farther than I expect before my knees give out beneath me, and I collapse against the wall.

My sister kneels next to me. "Stay with me, Odette."

I only shake my head. "Please go," I whisper, but a shadow passes over us, a broad figure emerging from around the corner of the stone building. A man on horseback who's leading another horse at his side.

Samuel. He hasn't left me yet. The men's screams must have led him here too. Climbing down, he examines me, collapsed on the cobblestone, my muscles slack, my eyes glazed over.

"You're in no condition to ride back," he says flatly.

Freya stares at him. "Well, she can't stay. Not with every witchfinder in the capital looking for her."

But I already know beyond reason what Samuel means. I can't ride back on my own, so he's ready to leave me behind.

"The herbs?" he asks, his voice like iron against bone. "Where are they?"

The one thing I'm good for. I try to inch backward, but he advances on me, his shadow devouring my body. With a swift motion, he forces his hand into my front pocket. The same pocket where the spell bottle shattered. A piercing yowl like a feral cat, and he recoils, bits of broken glass embedded in the tips of his fingers.

His jaw sets, thin rivers of blood leaking down his hand. "Give me what Anna needs."

I clutch my jacket tighter, the bottle of herbs heavy inside. There are voices all around, and the men have almost reached us now.

"We don't have time for this," Samuel says, and his fingers spasm toward his boot, toward the dagger he's kept in there since Anna and I were girls. "Just give me the herbs, Odette."

I grit my teeth. "No."

My sister gazes up at the skyline, this place where she belongs now. Then she looks back at us. "I'll come with you," she says. "I'll ride her home."

Samuel grimaces at this, eager to argue, but with the voices drawing nearer, he blots his bloodied hand on his worn trousers and climbs back onto his horse. I pull myself up onto the palfrey, drooping over him, my arms wrapped awkwardly around his neck, and my sister scrambles onto the saddle behind me and takes the reins.

"I'll get you home," she whispers, and together, we ride out of town, the horses heaving and galloping fast. At the mouth of the capital, echoes of the witchfinders are everywhere, seeping into my veins. I'm not sure now if they're really here or only in my mind, the choir of their ungodly voices calling out my name, cursing that they let me get away again.

We pass through the gates, away from this city and back onto the road. Hope rises up inside me, and my head lolls against my sister. She winces at my touch, and I wrench away.

"I'm sorry," I whisper, as the sun dips lower in the sky, the horizon fading to a sallow yellow.

I grip the horse a little tighter. In my pocket, the satchel that Beatrix prepared for me is empty. I used the last of the salt in the Wharf District. Now there's no barrier between us and the darkness, nothing to protect us if we can't make it back before sunset.

Though Samuel tries to outrun us, my sister is fast, so we stick together. On the back of Samuel's horse, the little girl hums a lullaby out of tune, and my skin tightens on my bones, but Samuel keeps riding, his back stiff as a corpse, his gaze set on the road ahead.

"He can't see the little girl, can he?" Freya whispers.

I shake my head. "For a while, I didn't think anyone could see her but me."

As though she can hear us, the little girl turns and smiles at me and my sister. Freya shudders but says nothing else.

We pass through silent villages on the road, shutters latched tight, doors locked and barricaded. There are no faces like before. The streets abandoned and dusty, there could be no one left at all.

The horses dash on, the darkness nearer now, and I choke on air, convinced this is it. We won't make it back. Then with the last of the sun vanishing in the sky, the village finally comes into view, and I exhale a laugh, harsh as sandpaper because I've never been so happy to see this place in my life.

The shadows shimmering around us now, we ride through the square. It should be quiet at this hour, but there are people everywhere, whispering and gazing down the roads, around corners, up into the hilltops.

I wonder what they're looking at, but we don't have time to find out. We keep going, along the cobblestone streets and up toward Samuel's stable, all the other horses dozing in the near dark of the evening.

Beatrix is waiting for us at the front window of the cottage. In an instant, she emerges in the alley, and she's not alone. There are three women at her side. The clerk from the general store, the blacksmith's wife, the schoolteacher. Beatrix whispers her thanks to them, and they squeeze her arm and say goodbye. Freya watches with me as they pass by, returning home before it's dark.

These girls who used to be our friends. They must have come to help Beatrix with Anna.

I want to thank them too, but Samuel seizes up on his horse, right next to the front door, his face pale and clammy.

"Odette?" He gazes at me, and for the first time, he just looks like a scared father. "Will you give me the herbs now?"

Now that we're back, there's no more damage he can do, no way to hold this over me, so I reach into my jacket lining and pass the herbs to Samuel. He climbs down from his horse, the bottle from the apothecary clutched tight in his hand, the most precious possession he's ever owned.

"It's exactly what you asked for," he says and forces it toward Beatrix.

She waves him into the house. "Start crushing everything in a mortar and pestle," she says. "I'll be right there."

She inches farther toward the road, nodding at Freya like we'd been expecting her. She nods at me as well before looking past the both of us at something in the distance. My feet heavy beneath me, I slip off the horse, following her gaze. There's movement on all the hills.

"I've been watching them for almost an hour," she says.

A fire gleams on the road beyond the trees. A bonfire with tiny figures warming themselves around it. They're miles away, but I shiver anyhow.

"Is it them?" I ask finally. "The witchfinders?"

She nods, still watching the flames on the hillside.

My whole body goes suddenly cold. "How many?"

Beatrix turns to me now, her eyes whirlpooling. "All of them."

chapter nine

THEY'RE COMING FROM EVERY DIRECTION. EVEN IN THE GATHERING DARK, you can see them, the hills crawling as if overrun by roaches. There's a group from the west, their campfire burning bright along the road. Others from the east, perched along the edge of the forest where the trees are still eager to devour them whole. If only they had the chance.

There are even a few stragglers here and there, figures dotted across the landscape like the inverse of a constellation, dark stars in a universe they own.

Though none of them are more than a few miles away, they aren't moving any nearer to us. The caravans must all be bedded down for the night, the lone witchfinders curled in ditches, their cloaks and their rage more than enough to keep them warm.

"What are they doing?" My flesh prickles in the cold. "Why not invade now?"

Beatrix shakes her head. "They must be waiting for something," she says, "or someone."

The doyen. They're holding back until their leader arrives. I imagine him traversing the same roads we just crossed, his face twisted, his horse rearing up. The other villages that we passed through are surely pulling their shutters a little tighter, clutching their children a little closer, praying that he doesn't stay, doesn't stop, doesn't rip their lives to pieces the way he'll soon do to us. This man who has eyes everywhere and ears that are always pricking up and listening to him, all his commands, all his latest whims.

Freya shivers. "How did the capital already get word to all these men?"

"I don't know," Beatrix says, but we've run out of time to stand here and watch them. The shadows are swirling around us, cobbling themselves together, their whispers heavy on the wind.

My head down, I sneak inside the house, staying close to Beatrix, like I'm an appendage of hers, something Samuel can't deny.

He glares at me anyhow. "Haven't you done enough?" he asks, his words soaked in venom as though I haven't done anything at all, as though I didn't risk my life to save his daughter.

I don't answer him. With Freya behind me, I keep following Beatrix who takes the mortar and pestle from Samuel and moves past the flickering hearth.

Anna is in her own room now, back where she belongs. Only nothing about this place feels safe anymore. The scent of the witchfinder lingers, heavy and oppressive like musk and burnt flesh. I want to scrub down every crevice of this house, a wilted rag in my hand, wearing down my own skin to an angry pink just to expel his memory from here. Not that it would matter. These walls might never be free of him now.

Beatrix drifts toward Anna as does Freya, but I hesitate in the doorway, my insides weak and twisted, this day still lingering in my bones. My hands numb, it aches me to admit that Samuel's right—there's nothing more I can do. No magic I have left to offer. No purpose here at all.

For his part, Samuel's more than prepared to push me out. He shoves past me, careful not to brush against me, his shadow casting a gray pall over his daughter's face. I inch farther into the room, but he tosses me a look that sears right through me, reminding me this is his home, and he can expel me anytime he likes.

Beatrix must know this, must see the dread blooming behind my eyes, because she regards him now, her hands never tiring, never stopping from her work.

"You've done enough for tonight," she says to him. "Off to bed. Rest your bones."

Samuel's body broadens. "I won't leave my daughter," he says.

With a soft smile, Beatrix reaches out and pats his arm. "I'm not giving you a choice, Samuel."

He opens his mouth, ready to argue, but he knows it's useless. Beatrix is the one who can help Anna. What she says tonight goes. His hands curled into ugly fists, Samuel curses to himself, and I think how if he were a witch, we'd all have been hexed and in the ground long ago. It's a blessing that some men have so little power.

When he reaches the doorway, he seizes up next to me. "And Odette?" he asks.

"She's staying," Beatrix says. "Now go on. We don't have much time."

One more grunt from him, guttural and childlike, and the door shuts behind him with a sullen thud. At this, something outside the window giggles.

I look toward the darkness, a wagon wheel lurching just beyond the gloom. There's a patter of tiny hands on the glass, echoing everywhere and nowhere at once, and a whisper breaks through the walls.

"Odette." This sound like fingernails raking across raw flesh. "Let us in."

I tell myself not to listen. As Freya gazes out into the shadows, her eyes wide and curious, I watch Beatrix instead. In her hands, the mixture has become thick and strange like colorless sap, oozing out of a bisected tree trunk. The spell is almost ready. I steady myself, preparing for what we're about to do, but no matter how much I try to ignore it, the darkness keeps beckoning to me, so loud it's nearly deafening.

"It's all right," Beatrix says, never glancing outside, never giving the shadows that much power over her. "I poured another salt ring around the house today. You're safe here."

Or as safe as I can be anywhere. The whispers outside never falter, and I grimace away, turning toward the closed door, my eyes blurring out and focusing again. There are marks around the doorway, splinters along the frame where someone kicked and scratched and did their best to escape. The witchfinder must have been busier in here than we realized.

One last turn of the mixture, and Beatrix looks up at me. "It's your turn," she says. "I need you to finish this."

"Me?" I gape at her. "Why?"

"Because," she says and passes me the mortar and pestle, "you're the only one who can."

Me. The witch that outlasted death, the one that can disintegrate a witchfinder or let a hex pass from her lips easier than a prayer. Beatrix must think that all this decay inside me means I can heal too.

A knot twists in my throat. "And what if I do it wrong?"

Beatrix smiles. "You won't."

Freya huddles closer to Beatrix. "You're good at this, Odette," she says. "You always have been."

I only hope they're right. I hold the spell steady in my hands, drawing up what's left in me. There isn't much there, my body almost too tired to stand. There are proper ways of doing a spell like this. Rituals for healing and protection, intricate incantations my mother taught me. Her voice simmers in me, reminding me how reckless I am, how I never cast a spell the right way.

You'll kill her, I hear her say inside my head. *Your witchcraft will kill your only friend.*

Biting down so hard my teeth crack, I chase my mother from my thoughts and focus on Anna. "Be well," I whisper, and my hands start to burn. "Be well and return to us."

Hovering near the bed, I use the end of the mortar so that I never touch Anna, and I paste the concoction onto the wound. It drips down her skin and deep into the gash like honey filling up a comb. The magic starts to unfurl from inside my body, the room tilting around me, a wave of heat enveloping us, and the things in the gloom must see this as an opening. They whisper louder now, their voices thrumming into my bones, right down to the marrow, every fiber in me humming with them. My skin pulls and scalds on my bones as if I'm being flayed alive, and the window bows inward, contorting harder this time, the glass spiderwebbing at the edges.

Freya and Beatrix cluster together next to me as Anna murmurs to herself, her body coiling tighter. On her arm, the ointment is fading to a dismal green, the color of rotting seaweed. She twists against the bed, her fingers clenching into fists, everything in her contorting.

"Anna?" My voice dissolves in an instant like snow on hot stone. She writhes again, and I let out a strangled sob because I'm sure she's slipping away from us, away from everything. This is my fault. I'm blighting her worse than the infection.

My hands shake, and I'm desperate to take it all back, desperate to do anything, but steady as the seasons, Beatrix holds me back, her arm stretched out in front of me, blocking my way without a single touch.

"Don't," she says.

"But it's killing her." I can barely breathe. "*I'm* killing her."

Just like my mother said that I would.

But Beatrix shakes her head. "No, you aren't," she says. "It's working, Odette. Trust yourself."

I close my eyes and focus again, letting the rest of the magic unfold from me.

It's been so long since I've done this, since I've healed someone. Another fleeting moment of Anna's pain, and something shifts in the room, everything quieter now. The heat around us recedes, and Anna settles back in her bed, a flush in her cheeks. Beatrix kneels at her side, running one hand over Anna's forehead, and without a word, I know it: the fever has broken.

"Thank you," Beatrix says. "Now we need to let her rest. And both of you should rest too."

Unlike Samuel, Freya and I won't argue with Beatrix. Our bodies weak from the day, we shuffle into the next room, and Beatrix closes the door quietly behind us. Here I am still in this home where I'm not welcome, this place I can't escape. There's no point in trying to leave now. With the witchfinders stationed everywhere on the roads, I couldn't make it past them. And then of course, there are the things waiting right outside for me.

My sister stares through the window. "How long have they been after you?"

I shrug. "Long enough," I say. "And they're getting stronger."

"Since the witchfinder came back?" she asks, and though I say nothing, she already knows she's right.

We linger, me at the window, Freya plopping down in the rocking chair.

"Those three women who were here when we arrived," she says. "The ones helping Beatrix. They were witches once, weren't they?"

"For a moment," I say, and I realize I still don't remember their names. I still don't remember a lot of things.

"Do you think they could help us?" she asks. "That maybe they could cast spells to ward off the witchfinders?"

"I doubt it," I say. I can't imagine they've held onto any of the magic I taught them. Witchcraft was only a passing diversion to them, and besides, that might as well have been another lifetime ago.

Samuel grumbles in the other room, his voice carrying through the whisper-thin walls. I watch his door, waiting for him to come crashing through it, demanding answers, but he stays inside his bedroom for now.

"Don't let him bother you." Freya nestles down in the rocking chair, drawing up a moth-gnawed blanket around her. "This isn't your fault."

I wish I could believe that. For years, I'd kept myself from hexing anyone, from hurting anyone. Yet today, I would've happily watched the birds tear all the witchfinders to pieces in the Wharf District. What I wouldn't have done to witness those soulless men squirming and wheezing for help, their flesh ripped from their bones, their eyes plucked out of their skulls like moist olives. My mouth practically waters thinking about it.

"I'm afraid," I whisper suddenly, and Freya peers at me through the dark.

"Of what?" she asks.

"Of myself."

She lets out a heavy laugh. "That's not so bad," she says. "There are worse people to be afraid of."

Freya pulls her knees tight into her chest, and with the rocking chair creaking beneath her, she's asleep in a minute. I listen to her snore, the rhythm so familiar that it's almost like a lullaby. Almost like before, when we'd curl together in the same shabby bed, the rope beneath our mattress threadbare, our thin comforter frayed at the corners.

"Can we run away tomorrow?" she'd whisper to me, her fingers entwined with mine, and I'd hold her close.

"Soon," I'd say, a lie I never meant to tell.

All night, I stay awake, watching out the window, long tendrils of smoke pushing at the edges of the glass, spectral whispers ricocheting about the room. I promise myself I can keep them out. I can stop all of this. But that means I can't close my eyes or let down my guard. That's when they'll get in.

It's nearly dawn when the door to Anna's bedroom creaks opens, and Beatrix is there, her figure gauzy in the vague light of morning.

I jolt to my feet. "How is she?"

"Holding steady," Beatrix says, but from the quiver in her voice, not steady enough.

I exhale a thin breath. "Is there anything else I can do?"

"We need something to keep her grounded while the spell finishes," she says. "It doesn't have to be much. Something small, something that she loved or that reminded her of home."

Home. Not this place then. She was always more at home in the forest than in this cottage.

I hesitate. "I might have something that will work."

It's across town in the ash. In the growing sunlight, I steal through alleys and across backyards to get to it. To get back home.

The skeleton of my childhood is waiting for me on my old street, the rafters splintered and collapsed. I haven't been inside this house since there was still a house to stand in. What I'm looking for could have been singed away that night in the fire. I won't know for sure until I take these last few steps and sift through the cinders.

I close my eyes and cross the threshold.

All the way in the back in what's left of a windowless room, I find the place where it should be. Beneath the burnt outline of the bed where Freya and I would curl up tight and hide away from the world. My hands plunge into the ash, searching for Anna's jar of feathers. This talisman of our lives before, of birds and magic and secrets only girls can share.

I keep digging, but there's movement at the corner of my eye, something darting this way and that. The children are here, blurring past me. They're pulling the wagon behind them, and it's filled with bits of dirt and something else, though they're moving too quickly for me to see what it is.

The little girl appears next to me, no more than a few feet away, lingering on the other side of the charred foundation. "Good morning, Odette."

"Hello again," I say, and she paces back and forth, me on the inside, her on the outside.

"I told you we should have left." She glances toward the hills, still teeming with men, their bonfires blackened in the night. "It's too late now."

"I guess so," I say, doing my best to ignore the children pushing closer at the edges of my vision.

"And the game is almost over too." She flashes me a sad smile. "We'll miss you."

I squint at her. "Where are you going?"

"We're not going anywhere," she says, and the other children are suddenly in a line around her, their faces swirling, their chubby fingers curling into claws. I try not to stare. They don't make any more sense when I look directly at them anyhow.

"You were outside last night at Anna's window," I say, still searching the ash, my hands chapped and aching. "You need to leave her alone. All of you."

The little girl scrunches up her nose. "But we like Anna. We won't hurt her."

My fingers trembling, I feel it at last. The cold glass jar. I extract it from the wreckage of my home, and there it is inside—the bundle of feathers, bright and safe and untouched by the flames.

"And what about me?" I ask, my lips dry. "Will you hurt me?"

"*I* won't." The little girl folds her hands in front of her. "But the rest of us aren't so sure yet."

The wagon is abandoned behind the other children, and I see now what's inside. The crow, *my* crow. He's hooded and tethered to the handle like a falcon, and I wonder how many times he's tried to take off into the sky. Maybe to escape them or maybe to return to me.

"Why would you want to hurt me?" I ask. "What good would that do?"

The little girl laughs, her mouth barely moving. "You know all those bedtime tales about witches who dine on children? How it gives them power?" She nods at her strange friends. "They think maybe it works the other way around too."

They're everywhere now, swarming all around me. The whites of their eyes gobbling up the irises, everything about them ready to gobble me up too. I back away, ash dancing in the air, glass shards digging into the soles of my boots. But they can't move past the edge of the foundation. The spell I cast years ago is holding strong.

I wheeze out a soft sob. "Do you hate me?"

The little girl winces as if injured by the question. "No," she says. "Of course not."

"Then why are you doing this?"

Her eyes dark, she shakes her head. "Because we have to," she whispers.

"Who told you that?" I stare at her. "Who's doing this?"

She won't look at me now. "I can't tell you."

I want to plead with her, demand for her to divulge everything, to tell me who's in the shadows every night with her, but a voice rises up behind me. "Odette?"

I whirl around. The girls I grew up with are standing where my front door used to be. The clerk from the general store, the blacksmith's wife, the schoolteacher, right there on the street where they used to meet Anna and me. They join me in the wreckage of my home, the hems of their gowns stained with ash, and I fold my body tighter into itself, careful not to touch them, not to remind them of why they fear me. When I look around, the children are gone, chased off by this unexpected company, not so much as a creak of the wagon left in their wake. Now I have to deal with my past instead.

"What can we do? How can we help?" the three of them ask, their voices overlapping. "What can we do about these men?"

I gape at them. After all this time, now they want my advice. Nothing about this should surprise me. This is how it's always been. People come to witches for favors, demanding hearts be mended, fortunes righted. They never bother with us otherwise. Nobody worries about the witch, about how lonely a cottage tucked away in the forest can be. It's as if we're made of magic and nothing more.

"What about the spells you taught us?" they ask. "Would those help?"

I nearly laugh in their faces at that. Like I said to Freya last night, I can't imagine they remember anything I showed them. They were so quick to discard it, to discard me and Freya and Anna when their families told them to.

"Sure," I say because I'll do anything right now to make them leave me alone. "Those spells would help. Why don't you all go home and practice?"

They hesitate. "Then what?"

"Then we'll figure out what to do when those men arrive."

They look ready to argue or certainly ready to ask more questions, but I don't have time for this. I need to get back, I need to help Anna, so I step over the blackened foundation and move into the street, not saying another word.

Back in Anna's room, Beatrix is preparing another poultice, and I give her the feathers.

"Thank you," she says. Her hands unsteady, she removes them from the jar and tries to balance them on the top of the headboard, but they won't stay put, fluttering limply to the floor.

"I've got something that will help," I say and reach into my jacket. The knotted-up ribbon from my pocket. This compulsion, this way I've stopped myself from doing magic. I don't need it anymore, so I loop it around the ends of the feathers and hang the whole bundle from the bedpost, right there where it might be the very first thing Anna sees when she wakes up again.

Beatrix smiles. "It's perfect," she says, her voice as comforting as warm grog.

When I return to the hearth, Freya stirs in the rocking chair, rubbing her eyes like a weary child. "How's Anna?"

"Alive," I say, and that word feels so good to speak aloud.

"And the men?"

"Still out there."

Freya stares into the fire, her eyes colorless and unfocused. "We should run," she whispers. "At least to the forest. Wait this out."

I shake my head. "And what about Anna? We can't leave her here."

"We have to do something." Freya hesitates. "Is there maybe a spell that Mama taught you?"

I scoff. "There are all kinds of spells," I say, but none of them ever worked, not for me. Magic our mother's way was always painful and cruel.

But Freya is watching me now, her face pinched and scared, and I have to do something. So I try anyhow. Murmuring an old incantation, I reach out toward the fire and ask the flame to dance. Just a little, just enough for me to believe that maybe I've got something left in me to stop these men. My fingertips numb, the flicker in the hearth burns on, ignoring me altogether. This body of mine might be made of fire, but between yesterday in the capital and last night with Anna, I'm too exhausted for it to matter.

Freya doesn't have the strength either. Curled up in the rocking chair, her skin is wan, everything in her drained from yesterday's journey.

"I didn't want to come back to this village at all," she says, almost to herself. "I certainly don't want to stay here and die."

This twists deep in my heart. She never planned to return, but she did, all because of me. And I brought her back home to a place more dangerous right now than even the capital. I start to say something else, an apology maybe, but in the next room, Samuel rises from bed and staggers bleary-eyed through the doorway. The morning has begun, one that already feels like the last.

The day passes slow and strange. A shared pot of oatmeal for breakfast, tasteless soup for lunch, our eyes always on the windows. We do our best to pretend this is a normal day mostly because we can't think of anything else to do. Samuel tends to the horses, and Beatrix tends to Anna who's drawing ever nearer to us. With the witchfinders drawing nearer too, I wonder what kind of world will be waiting for her when she awakens.

Every hour, I creep back to the hearth—to conjure a spell, to coax the flames, to do anything at all—but I'm still hollowed out inside, and nothing's working the way it should. The men will be here soon, and I can't stop them. I could try to cast a protective spell around the house like I did when I was young, but it wouldn't help. The witchfinders would just burn us alive the same way they did to my parents. If they want in, there's no way to keep them out.

A bitter thunderstorm ushers us into the afternoon, and my sister and I join Beatrix and Samuel at the table, the four of us eating supper together in sullen silence, listening always for a rapping on the door or a gentle whir of flames in the town square. All the melodies the witchfinders bring with them to a village.

With evening draping over us, I sit by the window, watching for their arrival.

"What's taking them so long?" Freya asks, but all I can do is shake my head. We made that trip in only a few hours. The doyen should have been here by now.

I leave the others to check on Anna. Her eyes bright, she looks up at me.

"Hello," she says.

I smile. "Hello again."

Outside, it's dark now, and the gloom is moving closer, my bones humming beneath my skin.

It'll be fine. They'll stay out tonight. That's what I tell myself. But as I kneel next to Anna, still smiling at her, my throat closes up, and I hear it: the rain still streaming down the house, washing away the day.

Washing away the salt circle.

The house lurches around us, and the shadows are everywhere at once—pushing under the windows, slipping between the walls, sinking deep in my skin, my guts, my marrow.

Her face ashen, Anna reaches out for me. "Odette?" She says my name as though it might tether me here, but it's already too late. The world is cascading away from me, and everything around me fades to black.

I open my eyes, and my hands are in the earth, wrenching bones from the darkness. I'm back in the graveyard, and when I stumble to my feet, dread clenches inside me because I realize I'm not alone.

Black boots, black cloaks, those vile grins that never fade. The witchfinders have come down from the hills at last.

And they're standing all around me.

chapter ten

There are more men than I can count in the dark. Dozens of them, maybe even a hundred. They grunt and spit and exhale their hideous laughs like braying mules, one hand on the knives dangling from their belts, the other free and ready to take hold of a wrist, an arm, a throat.

My breath escapes me, and I tip my head up to the sky. There are bits of moonlight, enough to see flashes of the men's faces but almost nothing else. I want to try and run, but they're everywhere, blocking the paths, their bodies broad and unforgiving. They lean over the fence, all eyes looking straight through me.

"Is she whispering to those bones?" one of them asks.

Another witchfinder nods. "They say she whispers to ghosts too."

"That's good," the first says with a glint of a grin, "since she'll soon be one herself."

I sneer back at them. "I could curse every one of you," I whisper, but it isn't true. I'd never be able to destroy this many. If I tried, it would only destroy me.

Other voices murmur as well, reaching out from the earth, but in the gloom, I can barely tell the phantoms from the witchfinders. All I know is they've got me outnumbered.

Then the moon shifts in the sky, and I see something else. These men have surrounded me, but even though they don't realize it, they're surrounded too. The children are here, their figures nebulous like splotches on a canvas, their lips pulled back in feral smiles. At the end of the line, those familiar wheels screech, and everything in me seizes up.

The wagon is filled with bones now.

I look down at my soil-drenched hands and at the hole like a gaping wound I've dug into the ground. I'm poised before a grave, one that's empty. These children followed me, and they're collecting the charred body that I yanked up out of the gloom.

Why would I do this? Why is the darkness directing me here? My legs unsteady beneath me, I gaze at all the men watching with their harsh, inquisitive eyes. The children watch me the same way. I want to run again, but something else happens instead. It stirs within me, that need to escape, to take flight.

In spite of myself, my body starts to rise. I don't know if I'm the one doing this or if these shadows are lifting me up, taking me away from here.

I drift further into the air, but below me, the witchfinders aren't impressed. On the ground, they snicker and wave goodbye.

"We'll find you wherever you go," they call out as the world dissolves.

It's past dawn when I awaken on the street, my hands numb, my fingernails limned with earth.

I'm back in the village, right in the middle of the town square. The darkness could have taken me anywhere. I could have left this town, this county, this kingdom. Yet here I am, deposited back in the center of a place that I can't seem to escape.

A line of horses snuff past, their liquid eyes seeing nothing except what the men tell them to see. Even more witchfinders have arrived now, scattered across the streets like wedding rice. I close my eyes, and I can sense them all around me. They're in the school, they're in the shops, they're quartering in the rows of houses, choosing the chair at the head of the table, nestling down in the daughters' beds.

At the tavern, they stuff themselves with gruel and mead and beef barley by the bucketful, always cursing and calling out to one another like quarrelsome brothers.

I pull myself up, and in the street, I stumble by the other villagers as they shuffle home, the lines deeper around their eyes, their complexions gone dull. They stare into my face, their eyes silently pleading with me as though I can fix what's happened. As though I can somehow save us from these men. But I was never chosen for this. My hands never wrenched a sword from a stone. There was nothing I did that was right and good and needed in the world. It was what I couldn't do that mattered: this body that wouldn't burn.

The army of witchfinders, the giggling children, the figures in the gloom—everything is drawing closer to us. And drawing closer to me, the witch who should be dead. Maybe it would be best if I just ran, even if they catch me on the road and rip me to pieces. At least that way, Beatrix and Anna and Freya might be safe.

A towering wagon stops next to me, and it's packed to the brim with wooden planks and dry straw, sepulchers ready to be assembled. The town square is already covered in pyres, and the men are still at work on more.

I try to back away, but the witchfinder driving the wagon glances down at me. He grins and nods at the mounds of straw.

"Do you like what you see?" he asks, and I hate him a little bit more.

"Why bother with all of this?" I glare up at him. "I don't think there are this many witches left in the whole world."

Another flash of that ugly smirk. "You can't be too sure," he says.

But they can be sure. By the time they're done, there won't be anyone left to burn.

Above us, the sky is the color of damp gunpowder, the sun hidden behind a tangle of clouds. The morning will soon slip away, and by the looks of it, the doyen still hasn't arrived. They're starting the festivities without him.

"Don't worry," the man says as if peering right through me. "He'll be here soon enough."

I grit my teeth. "I didn't ask about him."

"No," he says, "but you didn't have to. I bet you're always thinking of him, aren't you?" He leans in closer, and the stink and sweat of his body gag me. "Do you even dream of him sometimes? This man that filled you up with fire?"

It takes everything in me not to spit in his face. "You stayed up in those mountains for two days," I say. "Why aren't you waiting on him now?"

"But we are," he says, his face brightening. "Why do you think we haven't arrested you yet?"

This wallops me right in the chest. Their plan unfurled before me. The doyen rises up like smoke in my mind, licking his lips, eager to do the honors of murdering me himself.

My head spun, I stagger away from the pyres, rushing past the tavern where you can hear the witchfinders bellowing inside, this whole village theirs for the taking now. I still don't know how they're getting word from the capital, but only one thing matters: the doyen will be here soon. And when he arrives, we can't be anywhere in his warpath.

Back at Anna's house, I shove open the front door and stumble inside, nearly collapsing on the floor.

In a flash, Beatrix is at my side, always at the ready with an herb compress or a tincture meant to solve all your woes. And that's exactly what she used to do. If only it was the same now.

"Are you hurt?" she asks, the lines around her eyes graver than before, and I shake my head, barely able to speak, still queasy from speaking to that witchfinder.

Beatrix ushers me to the rocking chair and kneels at my side, the same way she did years ago when I had a skinned knee in need of mending.

"I was worried you weren't coming back," she whispers, and I know what she really means. She was scared I was gone, dissolved into the shadows, not so much as a pile of dust to bury. I wonder what it looked like when the darkness ripped me from this place last night. Did it pull me through the front door or out a window? Or did it simply turn me to mist, as insubstantial as a shadow?

I search the empty room. "Where's Freya?"

Beatrix hesitates, cupping her hands together in front of her. "She left this morning. She didn't tell me where she was going."

This aches in my heart, but I should have expected it. She probably went back to the capital, to the place she calls home now. Seeing her sister torn away in the darkness must have been too much for her. I only hope she managed to make it past the witchfinders without being seen.

"And Anna?" I ask. "Is she any better?"

"A little."

"Better enough?" I ask, peering at Beatrix, and instantly, she understands me. Anna was the one thing keeping us from running yesterday, but now maybe, we can all make it to the forest.

"She could be ready by evening," Beatrix says, but I shake my head.

"I can't wait that long."

It isn't safe for me in the night. The shadows are getting stronger. They used to only whisper in my ear, tugging at me, their bristly fingers lashing at my face. Now they can rip me from the ground where I stand, my body their own marionette. If I go out tonight, they're liable to consume me whole.

Samuel stirs in his bedroom, his feet heavy, a grumble lodged in his throat. He'll appear in the doorway any moment, eager to rebuke me before he's even had his slop and tea for breakfast.

My head down, I slip into Anna's room, daylight stealing in through the window smudges where the children have been. She's resting there in her bed, a quilt her mother made gathered up under her chin, her face pallid but breath steady. She's holding on. For how long, none of us can be sure, but she's here right now, and that's all that matters.

I crouch down next to her, squinting again at the window when my guts clench. Those tiny fingerprints, the ones the children made. They aren't on the outside of the glass anymore. They're on the inside now.

I should have thought of this sooner. If the darkness could get in, of course these children can too. They could be anywhere, one or two of them hiding in plain sight. Beneath the bed, tucked away like an heirloom. Clinging to the ceiling, their limbs as nubile as spider legs.

"Odette?" Anna says. She's peering up at me from beneath the heavy blanket.

I move closer to her, my gaze still darting about the room. "The children?" I whisper. "Where are they?"

"Oh, them?" A stifled nod of her head. "They're standing right behind you."

A giggle echoes off the walls. Everything twists inside me, and I don't want to look, but I already know it's too late to hide. I gather myself together enough to turn around, and there they are. A line of them against the wall, their eyes bleeding to white as they watch me.

"Get out," I say as though what I tell them will even matter. "You're not welcome."

Anna struggles to sit up in bed. "It's fine," she says, her voice rasping. "They've been keeping me company. They sang me lullabies, the same ones my mama used to know."

More like dirges. I stare at them, remembering the wagon last night, all packed up with goodies that aren't theirs to keep. "What are you doing with all the bones in the graveyard?" I ask.

The little girl tilts her head at me. "Exactly what you told us to do."

"But I didn't tell you anything."

"Yes, you did," she says, snapping her tongue. "You just don't remember."

The children advance on me slowly, and I motion Anna out of bed. She struggles to her feet, still wrapped up in the quilt, and the two of us inch away through the doorway and past the hearth. We keep going until we're on the far side of the house, Anna leaned against the wall, my back pressed into Samuel's desk where he keeps his letters and keys. Beatrix stands frozen near the window, her lips parted as if ready to scream. I hold up one hand, trying to steady her and trying to steady myself too.

"Why are you here?" I ask the children.

The little girl smiles. "Because we're not quite done with the game yet. Not until we show you something." She motions behind me. "It's right there, Odette. You'll find it in that desk drawer."

I shouldn't listen to her. For all I know, she's doing this on a whim, on a dare, for no reason at all. But she keeps watching me, and for some reason, I need to see where she's leading me. My hands fumble behind me in the drawer, and I find it there at once, right on top. A single letter written on cheap, yellowed paper.

Dear Uncle, it begins, and something deep in my belly writhes. This is from the would-be witchfinder, a letter he sent to Samuel. Perhaps the last letter he sent to anyone. My eyes skim over a list of banal niceties, the usual volley of family salutations, only to settle on the final lines there at the bottom. The only lines that matter.

I'll come to the village next week. Point out the witch to me, and I promise I'll solve both our problems.

It's so easy to envision how this happened. Samuel with his poison pen, scribbling letters back and forth to relatives until he finally got hold of a nephew who had just the wrong amount of ambition. A nephew that wanted to prove himself by dispatching a witch, and Samuel with a witch in need of dispatching.

"I'm sorry," he says, lingering in the doorway of his bedroom.

I stare back at him. "You," I say, the truth aching inside me. "You did this to us."

The letter droops in my hand, and he won't look at me, his face leeching of color, his mouth gone slack. For the first time in all the years I've known him, he's got nothing to say.

I back away, and Anna comes too, one careful step after another, thin slippers on her feet. It's not much, but it's better than being barefoot, especially since we'll have to run for it. Beatrix is already unlatching the front door as Samuel moves toward us, oblivious to the children all around him. The little girl laughs, and I'm suddenly not sure who I should be more afraid of—these miniature phantoms ready to devour me whole or a man who would serve up his own daughter on a witchfinder's platter.

I won't stay here and decide. Anna, Beatrix, and I edge through the door, and once we've all reached the alley, we turn and run.

Outside in the street, the men are busy at work. Their hammers striking and splintering wooden planks, their rough hands gathering together straw, their bodies blocking the dirt path that would have taken us the long way out of town. Still, they haven't noticed us yet, so we sneak through the alleyways, our feet slipping into the cracks between the chipped cobblestone. Maybe we can get to the main road. Next to me, Anna is gathered up in her mother's quilt, but she's still shivering. This journey could be enough to do her in, but we've got no choice now.

"Do you think you can make it?" I whisper to her, and she only nods.

Somewhere in the distance, I hear Samuel's voice, calling Anna's name. He'll be tracking us now too. Just like the witchfinders. Just like the children.

"What now?" Anna huddles near me and Beatrix in the alley. "How do we get past them?"

The men are there in the town square, so close I can almost hear their ragged heartbeats.

"The only way we can," I say. "By blending in with them."

I'm almost too tired to try this, but we're out of time and out of options. There's enough lingering power in me, this rage at Samuel's betrayal, so with my eyes closed and my hands burning, I conjure it up in me—black boots, black cloaks, those ugly grins. The perfect disguise. When I open my eyes, all three of us are gone, hidden beneath these vile facades.

Beatrix marvels at my shifted face before admiring her own new hands. "What have you done?" she asks.

"What I had to do," I say, ashamed at what I've made us.

It won't last. This much magic is heavy and bulging and strange, everything about it misshapen and unreal. If anyone looks too closely at us, they'll realize something's not right, but so long as we can get to the main road that leads directly out of the village, maybe we'll just look like three witchfinders gathering up supplies. Maybe we'll have enough time.

We start out into the street, all of us with our heads down. Nobody notices us. There are so many witchfinders, and they probably don't even all know each other's names.

Past the town square and down the last street, we head out of the village, and Anna smiles, though it isn't the same as her real smile. It's the smile of a witchfinder. I hate that we look like them. I hate wearing this even as a disguise. It feels like a betrayal.

We're almost to the crossroads, and everything in me is tearing in two. I'm ready to dissolve the glamour when another wave of witchfinders on horseback approaches us.

"Have they already started burning her yet?" one of them asks us.

I shake my head, my tongue still, not wanting my voice to give me away.

"Good to hear," he says and regards the others, his eyes flashing dark. "Maybe we'll each get a turn first."

A turn. Each of them having a go at me, all the different ways to tear apart a woman. I grit my teeth, and this time, I can't help myself. My face scrunched up, I spit right on his boot, resting in the stirrups, and that's all it takes. The glamour cracks in two and shatters around us, our faces exposed. All the men gape at us, not fathoming what just happened, and this moment of hesitation is enough.

"Run," I wheeze, and the three of us take off past the crossroads.

None of us are as fast as we want to be—Anna with her barely healed arm, Beatrix with her world-worn body, me with the residual magic weighing me down—but we can't stop. The men have turned their horses now, and they're coming right behind us.

"They're too close." Anna winces, the pounding of hooves at our heels.

I glance back once, and the horses are staring into us, their eyes seeing us, not hating the thought of us like the men do. My heart clenches, and I remember the spell I did when I was young, the one that the witchfinders never noticed but the horses did. Just like the birds who were always listening. Maybe these animals can hear me a little bit easier.

"Stop," I whisper to them. "Please. Make them stop."

At first, I think it's all for nothing. The men keep coming, their teeth gnashing, their nostrils flaring. But then a palfrey whinnies to the sky, and one after another, all the horses seize up, right down the line, their broad bodies strong and silent against the day.

The men spit and kick and curse, but it does no good. The horses won't budge.

Still swearing, the witchfinders leap from their saddles, ready to pursue us on foot, but at last, the edge of the forest comes into view. Breathless and weary,

Beatrix and Anna help each other along as I lead us into the thicket. It's the only way they won't be lost—with a witch to guide them. Although in a way, all three of us are witches now and always have been. I'm just the only one who remembers it.

We keep going into the woods, along the deer runs marked with my own footsteps, and into the clearing where my cottage stands sentry. The men scream behind us, but they can't follow. This is the one place they'll never be welcome.

The cold whips around us, and I force open the front door, beckoning Anna and Beatrix inside. In the corner, the restless spell bottles whisper their hellos, and I push the door closed behind us, latching it tight. Beatrix rests on my makeshift bed, her body curled into a crescent moon, a slight smile still on her face. It was a longer trek into the woods than she's used to, but she's still with us. We're all still together. Everyone except Freya. I wish she could have come too, but if she's headed back to the capital, that's probably better. It's certainly safer. After all, the witchfinders are all in our village now.

Snow murmurs against the window as softly as a coming plague, and Anna helps me coax a fire in the hearth.

"I'm sorry about Samuel," I say, and she gives me a half smile that looks liable to crumble into dust.

"It's not your fault." She gnaws her bottom lip until it's raw. "I should have expected it."

I watch her quietly. "Why do you say that?"

"Because he's always been like this," she says. "The night they arrested you, he locked me in my bedroom for hours. Told me it was for my own good. To keep me safe, he claimed, even though I tried to claw my way out."

The marks on the doorframe. Those weren't the work of the witchfinder at all. They were from Anna.

She warms her cold, colorless hands over the nascent flames. "By the time I could get to the forest, I'd already forgotten my way. And you were long gone." She shakes her head. "I tried to get back to you so many times. Anytime you'd come to town, I'd always wait on the street in front of your house like we used to do. But you never showed up. After a while, I figured it was your way of telling me to leave you alone."

Grief twists inside me. For five years, I've been convinced she abandoned me, and all that time, she thought I was the one who'd forgotten her.

There's a rustling outside, and our faces snap toward the window. The noise recedes, but it still doesn't feel as though we're entirely alone.

Anna shudders, draping her quilt around her shoulders like a heavy shawl. "Those children," she says. "My father couldn't see them, could he?"

I shake my head. "I think only witches can see them."

"Why?" she asks.

"Maybe because they're witches too," I say. "Or the children of witches."

"But where are their mothers and fathers?" Anna asks, nearly choking on her own words because she already knows the answer.

Missing witches are easy to account for. They're a tally mark in a ledger, an unclaimed blot of ash in a town square, a name that no one remembers except the family left behind. The little girl and her friends probably have nowhere else to go. That's why they're playing this game, directed by some unseen hand, the little girl as the emissary, the only one we can see clearly. The one I've told again and again to bury the bones.

We settle down in my barren cottage, the fire flickering brighter in the hearth. This place has never been much to speak of, but then, I've never tried to make it any better. Dust soaks through everything. I wipe away the grime from the floor, and when I withdraw my hand, there's something there. A single black feather glinting in the darkness.

Anna picks it up and turns it over in her palm. "The birds were here, weren't they?" she asks, and I nod.

"I don't understand why," I say. "After what I've done to them."

That spell I must have accidentally cast to make them tumble from the clouds.

But Anna only stares at me. "You didn't do any of this to them, Odette," she says. "The birds always came to us. To tell us their secrets and to warn us too. Don't you remember?"

"An omen," I whisper. That's why they fell from the sky. It was a harbinger that the witchfinders were returning. We just didn't realize then that's what the birds were telling us.

Maybe I've been wrong this entire time. Maybe I've been blaming myself for what I haven't done.

And then there are the things that are my fault. A voice cuts through the air like a knife, reminding me of my shame all over again.

My brother. What have you done to him?

The face in the locket, the witchfinder's sister. She surfaces within me, her words splintering through my body.

He's dead, isn't he?

I look to Anna. "Your cousin," I say. "He has a sister. What's her name?"

She hesitates. "Sara," she says finally. "How do you know about her?"

"I saw her in the capital," I say, never mentioning how I'd first met her days before that, her visage giving the spell bottle its power. I also don't mention how Sara is still whispering to me even now, that soft voice leaking into the room through every wall, her words warbling and dust-soaked, like a ghost that won't ever rest.

I hear other voices too. The witchfinders are drawing closer. They're still on the road and unable to breach the trees, their footfalls heavy, their tempers short. I turn away toward the window, and their voices thrum within me, the words tasting of ash and brine.

If we can't get to them, we'll coax them into coming to us.

I seize up, already feeling it in my bones even before I can see it. Not that we see it at all, not at first. It's the scent that overwhelms us. The stench of char and melting bark and leaves withering into dust.

Beatrix rises from my bed, her eyes widening, and next to me, Anna studies my face. "What is that?" she asks, and I want to scream because I know what they've done, how they're drawing us out like poison in a deep wound.

The forest. They're burning down the whole forest to get to us.

I was a fool not to have thought of it sooner. These men solve all their problems with fire. Why would this time be any different?

The heat draws closer, obliterating the desiccated remains of my herb garden. I close my eyes and wish the flames away, but they're too strong now. The fire is on the thatched roof, and it only takes a moment before it burns straight through, the walls of the cottage starting to buckle around us.

More flames descend, and I can feel it everywhere, the men shooting burning arrows through the trees, their aim impeccable, their cruel laughter rising to the sky. The door bows inward, the frame swelling and contorting, and there's no way out. We're cut off, trapped where the fire is only growing stronger.

Anna exhales a strangled scream. "What do we do?" she asks.

"I don't know," I say. The three of us cover our mouths, but the smoke is choking us, and we won't last long.

In the corner, a soft choir of whispers lilts in the air. The bottles. They're still here, still waiting. The half-finished wishes of all the witches that came before. I always felt these weren't my spells to touch, but maybe it simply wasn't the right time yet.

Forcing open the dusty hope chest, I scoop up all the bottles in my arms and pitch them one by one into the hearth. The glass heating up at once, they bubble and twist and exhale the sweetest laughter I've ever heard, so childlike and pure that, even out on the road, the witchfinders have to hear it too. It must make the men's blood boil that all their fire still can't suffocate the joy out of every heart.

With one final crystalline giggle, the bottles shatter into fragments, their edges reflecting all the light in this room and beyond. Their voices free, they rise up into the air, an uncanny aria, and the sheer force of them, the collective power of everything these women were, thunders through the walls and the window, toppling the door from its hinges. Daylight pours in, so bright it almost looks like a fire all its own. Beatrix grabs Anna by the hand and pulls her toward freedom.

They both reach out for me as well, but I don't follow them. Falling back, I imagine it—what it would feel like to stand here and let these flames consume me, the fire within mingling with the fire without, all of the heat encompassing my body at once, melting my flesh into the earth. How much simpler that would be. How much quicker than waiting on the witchfinders.

"Odette?" Anna's voice from the doorway. She's not moving, not escaping from this place like she should. Instead, she's waiting for me.

"Please go," I whisper, my voice gobbled up by the rush of flames.

But she won't leave, not without me. Neither will Beatrix, still lingering at Anna's side, both of their figures no more than gauzy outlines in the smoke.

The bricks in the hearth crumble inward. Everything is crumbling, and I hesitate for a long moment, still convinced that they'd be safer if I stayed behind.

"Come on now, darling." Beatrix's voice this time, steady as the tides, coaxing me to her as though I'm an errant child. In a way, I probably am, but she's never minded. She holds out her hand to me, and though I know I can't take it, I move toward her anyhow. The roof sagging above me, I step through what's left of the door and out into the light.

The cottage topples in on itself behind us, and together, we run, all of us wheezing and half-blind with soot, but there's almost nowhere left to go. We can't escape deeper into the woods. The men have made sure of that. The fire surrounds us in a V-formation, like migrating birds in flight, the flames leaving only a narrow path through the trees, one that leads directly back to the road.

And back to them.

The three of us burst through the burning forest, and the men already have their arrows aimed at us. Anna and Beatrix are still hand-in-hand with me trailing behind them, but as the witchfinders draw back their bows a little farther, I maneuver in front. It's me they want, and I'll make it easier on them. Maybe this way, they'll be so busy with me that Anna and Beatrix might get away yet.

Only there's one more now. The doyen is here at last, arriving in a grand spectacle, precisely how he likes it. All the witchfinders part around him, and he waltzes toward me like a spoiled king in a gilded court.

"Good evening, Odette," he says, his voice soaked with malice and propriety. He gives me that hideous gentleman's smile and tips his hat to me, the same way he always does. The other men draw nearer now, their shapes casting long shadows across my body.

This is it. That means I have nothing left to lose. With rage boiling over inside me, I grin back at him. And with my hands curled into claws, I lunge for his heart.

chapter eleven

MY HANDS ARE OUT, GRASPING FOR HIM, DESPERATE TO BRAND HIM WITH what he's done to me, these flames I can't escape. I get closer than I expect, my breath hot against his cheek, and he doesn't back away. As always, he just keeps smiling.

"Go on," he whispers as I press my splayed hand across his throat, his thick collar bunching up beneath my fingers, keeping me from searing straight into his skin.

The rest of the witchfinders charge forward, and I expect they'll take hold of me and wrench me away from him, but they do something worse than that. They seize Anna instead. A dozen men surround her, their arrows sharp against her neck, and she exhales an anguished cry like a rabbit in a snare. Beatrix tries to push to the front, tries to help, but the men hold her back as they stare into me.

I don't move. Neither does anyone else, not even as my hand sizzles through the doyen's sheepskin coat, ready to catch fire. Soon the whole jacket will be blazed away, and my skin will singe into his, our bodies so near that it sickens me. He'll finally know exactly what he's done to every women he's ever condemned. How fast the flesh will melt down to the bone and how fast the bone will melt too.

The doyen looks right through me, everything in his face brightening, and I can't tell if he's afraid or if he's rather enjoying himself. He motions at the other men, and they push their arrows a little deeper into Anna, drawing just enough blood to make her tremble.

"We'll slit her throat right here," he says. "If that's what you want."

I gaze at Anna, and gritting her teeth, she gives me the slightest of nods as though to signal me that it's all right. That she'd rather have me finish him even if that means they'll finish her too. This rage keeps rising up inside me, so thick and potent it nearly chokes me, but I can't let that happen. I can't let them have her.

"Let her go," I say, and with the doyen's jacket turning to char in my hand, I step away from him, my arms going slack at my sides. The other men heave toward me now, tossing Anna aside as though she's a useless trinket. A tangle of gloved hands sweeps over my body, shoving me to the dirt and pinning me beneath them. Their faces are a sea of nonsense, meaningless features, dead eyes. All except for him, the one visage I can't forget.

The doyen looms over me, inspecting every curve of my body. "You've always been too wild," he says, and it almost sounds as if he might like that.

At his feet, the men hold me down, their leather gloves melting against my skin.

"That's enough," he says. "I don't want to finish this here."

A wave of his hand, and that's all it takes. The men grumble and spit and climb off me. I struggle to my feet, my bones aching, and with the butts of their arrows, they force us along the road and back toward the village, Anna and Beatrix and me in the midst of them in this circle of witchfinders. This way, from every direction, they can always have their eyes on us and their weapons at our backs.

The sun is drooping in the sky, and all around us, ash and scorched leaves float through the air, the noxious scent of boiling bark filling up my lungs and suffocating the hope right out of me. The woods won't stop burning. They'll probably smolder through tonight and into tomorrow and maybe even into the next day. The witchfinders cough into their sleeves, their eyes watery, their throats raw, barely able to endure what they've done. I keep my gaze on the road, trying not to look up at what's left of my sanctuary. My home, my heart, scorching into nothing.

A part of me had always hoped the woods were like me, their skin impenetrable to fire, but thanks to these men, virtually everything is alight. Only a small ring of trees in the distance haven't burned. The Hyland Forest. As we pass by on the road, I swear I can almost hear it whispering to me, calling me closer, telling me to run into its embrace. As though it could be that simple. If we tried to escape now, there's no way we could make it that far. We could flee, but the witchfinders would pursue, and they'd cut out our hearts before we even had a chance to scream.

The doyen leers up at the Hyland Forest. "That part of the woods is a little like you, isn't it, Odette? It just won't do the polite thing and burn."

I say nothing, and next to me, Anna shivers.

"You should have let them have me," she whispers, the words souring in her mouth. "You should have finished him. That's what matters."

"No, it's not," I say. "You mean more than they do."

"None of us are going to mean anything soon," she says bitterly, and Beatrix shakes her head.

"Let's have none of that, all right?" she says, her voice as sweet as fresh honeysuckle, and for a moment, I can't help but smile. Then the men prod us forward, their blades nipping at our arms as we keep marching on.

At last, we cross into the village, a funeral procession in the making. Scared faces crowd around us, but there's nobody to help us and certainly nobody who cares. No Freya, no girls we used to dance with in the forest. The general store is all closed up, the windows dark, the door bolted. I wonder if they're inside, cowering in the back like they did that day with the birds. Some people can make an art out of running away.

At the corner, the children appear, all of them in a line, their wagon still filled with bones. These men move right past, still not seeing them, which is good. It gives the children a chance.

"Run," I mouth to the little girl, but she and her friends don't budge. They just keep standing there, their faces almost clearer to me now, their eyes so soft and sweet and almost scared. Not scared enough to flee though. They must be staying for a reason. Probably to finish their game. Probably because someone is telling them to.

We reach the tavern, and the brigade stops dead in the street. I peer up at the building, so much taller and gaunter than I ever remember it. I haven't been inside this place since I was a child dragging my father home, back when I was as scared and lost as I am now.

"Why are we here?" Anna whispers to me, but I don't have time to utter a word back to her. The men close in around us, kicking me out of the way, their hands all over Anna and Beatrix. My lips try to form a spell, anything to stop them, but there's no magic left to conjure inside me. My hands numb, I've worn myself out, and this time, I don't know how long it will take until I'll be ready again. That is, if I ever even get the chance.

Anna lets out a strangled scream as a pocket of witchfinders, impassive and cruel as an ocean torrent, carries off her and Beatrix. I reach out for them, but even if we were side by side, I still wouldn't be able to take their hands.

The doyen and a few of his men remain behind, still flocking around me, still keeping me from running.

"Where are they taking them?" I ask, panic slicing through my voice. "To the pyres? Are they taking them to the pyres?"

"Don't worry." The doyen snaps his tongue like an impatient schoolboy. "We've got plenty of time before my men get antsy enough to start any fires. Besides," he says and leans in closer, "when it does happen, I promise I won't let you miss it."

I back away from him. "And what now? What do you want with me?"

He smiles as the tavern door swings open before us. "After you," he says, and I'm desperate to run, though I know it doesn't matter. If I flee this place now, I'll never see Beatrix and Anna again. The doyen will make sure of that.

He extends his hand in front of him, inviting me in, and with my head up and eyes clear, I turn toward the door and cross the threshold into what's waiting for us.

Inside, the room is smoky and dim, only a row of pale taper candles to light our way. On a long, oak table, a banquet is awaiting us. Everything I could ever want is here: bulging links of blood sausage, candied cranberries, a plate of boiled eggs, a roast thick with fat and dripping in its own juices.

My breath halts in my chest because I understand what this is. A final supper. The same thing he offered the condemned women in the capital.

Only one thing is different from his parlor—there's another guest. I don't notice her at first, hidden there in the corner, blending in with the shadows as she watches me, her gaze dark, a curtain of red hair across her eyes.

The sister of the would-be witchfinder.

"Hello, Sara," I say, and she flinches at the sound of her name on my lips.

Witchfinders swarm about the room, omnipresent as a plague of locusts, and the door slams closed behind us. The doyen beams, his cheeks flushed, everything about him far too pleased with himself.

"So glad to see the two of you together," he says. "Sara here has become a valuable asset to us. Haven't you, love?"

He reaches out and pinches her chin, never bothering to notice how she winces away from him.

"Such a helpful girl," he continues. "I figured I should give you two a chance to meet before it's too late."

Before there's no more me, he means.

I can't understand at first why he's introducing us. Then Sara moves closer, her fingers clenching, and it's brimming there within her. The scent of power, swirling and contorting around us like smoke rings. Something primordial. Something dangerous.

"A witch," I whisper. "You're a witch."

That's how they got word to all the men strewn across the countryside. She tipped her head back and whispered to the sky, and they could hear her anywhere they went.

A witch in league with witchfinders.

The doyen steps between us now. "Let's finish our discussion over supper," he says and takes the chair at the head of the table. Sara slips into the seat next to his, her head down, and he smiles placidly at her because this is how he prefers his women—eager and loyal, more like hunting dogs than human beings.

"You don't have to do this," I say to her, but she doesn't even bother to look up at me. The two of them start in on the meal, their silverware clacking against bone.

The other men huddle nearby as the doyen and Sara gobble down the meat, juices dripping from their chins, sinews lodged between their teeth. Still standing, I twist toward the wall, refusing to sit with them. I've spent the last five years withering away, my stomach eternally raw with hunger, yet here I am with a feast before me, and I can't bear to take a single bite.

Not that I have to worry about this hunger or anything else for long. I wonder how he plans to do it this time. Will it be with flames, another pyre built just for me? Will I burn at all? Can I even die? Or will these men murder me a thousand times over, and I'll simply have to smile and live through it?

Outside on the street, there's an agonized holler and a fist pounding now at the door.

The doyen chuckles to himself and blots a spot of grease from his face. "It sounds like we have another guest," he says and motions to the other men. "Let him in."

A witchfinder unlatches the door, and Samuel erupts into the room, sweat soaking through his tattered jacket.

"Where is she?" His eyes are wild and colorless, the eyes of a madman, pinwheeling with grief. "Where's Anna?"

"She's alive." The doyen spoons three candied cranberries into his mouth, a splash of red staining his teeth. "It's the least we can do for you after all the help you've given us."

His face blazing, Samuel won't look at me. "I haven't helped you. I haven't helped anyone."

The doyen exhales a thick laugh. "Come now," he says. "Don't be modest. At the very least, you helped your nephew. Right up until the end, I suspect."

The doyen's gaze shifts to me, and my stomach churns as I remember that last moment in the house, there at the hearth. How the witchfinder must never have overtook Samuel at all.

"You helped him out of the bedroom," I say. "You let him go after Anna."

"No." Samuel's eyes on me now. "I let him go after you."

Me, the one that Samuel's wanted gone for years.

"I still don't understand," I say. "You said you were so afraid of these men coming back."

Samuel stares at the floorboards, creaking beneath us, not wanting to look the witchfinders in the face. "I was afraid," he whispers. "But I always knew they'd return. I knew they'd come back for you. And I figured if it was on my terms—"

His voice cuts out suddenly, and I can guess the rest. He thought he could control his nephew. Samuel, so petulant and cocksure, convinced he always knew best. When he finally realized what he'd unleashed, it was too late to stop it.

"But he didn't know who I was, not at first." I inch toward him. "Why didn't you tell him about me? That I was the witch he wanted?"

"Because," Samuel says, "Anna was suspicious the moment he arrived. If he'd arrested you right away, she would have known it was because of me."

I gape at him. "So you sent him after Beatrix instead?"

He shrugs like an admonished child. "I had to give someone to him."

Disgust scorches through me, and before I can stop myself, I slap him hard across the face, searing the outline of my hand into his cheek. The other witchfinders advance toward me, but Samuel holds up one hand to them.

"It's fine," he says. "I deserve it."

"You deserve worse," I say.

"So do you." He rubs his fingers across his burnt skin. "I only wanted to protect my daughter."

"Unfortunately," I say, "I don't think that worked out very well."

The doyen jolts from his chair. "That's enough for now," he says and ushers Samuel to the door, whispering poison and false promises in his ear. Probably all about how safe Anna is, how nothing bad will ever happen to anyone in this village. The beautiful lies that men like him can spin from nothing, straw into polished gold.

I can't bear to hear it, so I move toward the table where it's just me and Sara. I grip the back of the chair next to hers, my untouched meal glistening before me, the fat congealing and puddling in the middle of the plate.

"Why are you doing this?" I whisper to her. "Why are you helping them? They kill our kind."

"No," she says and gives me a cruel grin. "They kill *your* kind."

Me, the wrong sort of witch. Maybe that's what she truly believes or maybe that's what her brother said to her. How she was different—good and decent and whole, not a heretic like me. How he wouldn't burn her if he had the chance. Another man with another sweet lie, one he would have told her until the day he returned home with an order and a flame.

"I'm sorry," I say to her, and I honestly mean it.

She watches me, her eyes almost gray. "I feel like I know you. Like I've spoken to you many times in a dream." She hesitates. "Did you bewitch me?"

Shame seizes me, my face going hot. "Not on purpose," I say.

"But it was you?" she asks, leaning in. "Murmuring to me in the dark?"

"You spoke to me first."

"Not on purpose," she says, almost laughing to herself, and something passes between us. This enchantment inside us, this rage we share.

"Is it you?" I move closer to her. "Are you the one commanding the children?"

She stares at me. "What children?" she asks, one eyebrow twitching up, and though she could be lying, I know that she's not. She has no idea what I'm talking about. It must be someone else. Someone more powerful. And more vengeful.

With Samuel escorted back to the street, the doyen returns to the table and settles in to finish his meal. That's when I notice something. He and Sara each have a satchel dangling from their jacket pocket. It's a small bag, and I can tell from here what's inside. Several handfuls of salt.

Sara's been teaching him all her witch's secrets. That must have been what took them so long to arrive. I can imagine them in the capital after I escaped, colluding. Now he carries our magic with him, these little tricks he'd execute someone else for.

The doyen glances up at me, still standing, and motions to the empty chair across from him.

"Take a seat," he says. "Have your supper."

"No," I say, and here I am all over again, breaking this unspoken rule. Refusing a witchfinder. The other men storm toward me, their knives unsheathed, and fury festers up inside me. I should just be done with this. I should leap across this table and turn the doyen to ash and then let these men do the same to me. It would be so quick, and it would be irrevocably over.

Only that won't work either. There will still be all these witchfinders left, dozens of them clogging the streets, and with their doyen dead, they'd be out for blood more than before. This village probably wouldn't last the night.

Defeat fizzling inside me, I take the chair opposite his, and the doyen chortles.

"I know what you're thinking. How you'd like to leave me for dust the same way you did with Sara's brother." He leans back in his chair, a devious grin budding on his lips. "You and I aren't so different."

I glare back at him. "I'm nothing like you," I say even though I'm not sure that it's true. My mother's voice seethes inside me, and with my head spinning, I can't focus on anything. I can't even tell which thoughts in my head are mine anymore and which ones belong to someone else, to the shadows.

The doyen senses this in me, the way my resolve is withering. How pliable he must see me, like a knot of thick dough in his hands.

"Leave us," he says, and though his men open their mouths to protest, to stop him from being alone with me, they know better than to argue with their leader. I might not get to keep my neck, but they certainly want to keep theirs. The door closes with a dour thud behind them.

Sara, however, doesn't move. She just keeps working her way through her meal. A slice of boiled egg here, a pat of bright-yellow butter on a roll there, each bite more careful than the last.

The doyen observes her, a grimace settling over him before he nods toward the door. "Didn't you hear me?" he asks. "I'm sure they need you outside, Sara."

She stares at him. "For what?"

"I don't know," he says, and his whole face looks like a sneer. "Why don't you go and find out?"

Sara goes stiff as a corpse in her chair, and her gaze flits to me just long enough for me to see the fear blooming in her eyes. Then she's off, exactly as he commands. Up from the table and out the door into the street where the other men surround her.

The latch clicks behind her, and we're alone now, the two of us, me and this man made of nightmares. He's wanted me all to himself for years, and now he's got me. His captive audience. With a flourish, he fills a stone goblet with wine and slides it across to me. Never taking my eyes off him, I give it one swipe of my hand, and it topples off the table, the thick clay shattering into pieces, the liquid spraying red across the floor.

He laughs and pours wine for himself, quaffing it in an instant. "I call to you sometimes," he says and runs his tongue around the edges of his wet mouth. "Do you ever hear me?"

My cheeks burn. "No," I say, and he smiles.

"Liar."

I wish he were wrong. I wish I'd never heard his voice, that I'd forgotten all about him, but for all these years, he's never left me, not even for a moment.

"You said you were saving me for last," I say. "When would you have come back to make good on that promise?"

He hesitates before tipping his chin toward me, savoring this moment. "I wouldn't have," he says finally. "I always knew you'd come to me."

My body goes cold. "But I didn't," I whisper.

"Of course, you did," he says. "You came to me in the capital."

I shake my head. "I went there for Anna. Not you."

"Yet we found each other anyhow, didn't we?" He watches me, and I've never felt so seen and so shamed in my whole life. All this time, he's been drawing out this ordeal, waiting for me, waiting for years, because he knew all too well that he could afford to be patient.

He leans back in his chair, so comfortably smug it makes me nauseous just looking at him. "Sara's been a wonderful help to us," he says as though it's an afterthought, as though he hasn't been working up to this part all along. "You could do the same."

A laugh bubbles up in my throat. "And why would I ever do that?"

"Because," he says, "helping us is easier than dying."

My fingers clench into fists. "I wouldn't be so sure about that."

I'm prepared for him to argue with me, to bargain, to threaten, but he does something else instead. He rises from his chair and motions to the door.

"Walk with me," he says. "I'd like to show you something."

My fists still set on the table, I don't want to follow him. I don't want to do anything at all, certainly nothing that he commands. But when he opens the door, the men are congregating outside, ready to march back into this room and tear me from this seat, their leather gloves melting once more against my flesh. He's invited me to come with him, but we both already know I have no choice.

With my last shreds of courage, I too rise from the table, and together, we step through the door and out into the street. In the gathering twilight, everything has changed. The pyres are no longer confined to the town square. They're everywhere, winding along each road, tied up at every doorstep.

"Isn't it beautiful?" the doyen says as my heart seizes up in my chest. The witchfinders are ready to execute the whole village, one house at a time.

And the doyen is going to make me watch.

chapter twelve

I KEEP STARING AT THE PYRES, WISHING THEM AWAY, WILLING THEM TO DUST, but my hands are numb, the magic weak within me. After everything, I'm too tired to fight back just when the fight is the only thing that's left.

"You can't do this," I say finally, and the doyen laughs.

"Why not?" He circles me, his body twining around mine, so close we're almost embracing. "Everyone here has been protecting you. They're harboring a witch. That's a burning offense."

"A whole village?" The question nearly dissolves on my lips. "You'll kill a whole village?"

"I'll do whatever it takes," he says, and I know he means it. He and his men will make an example of us, a cautionary tale to be told in hushed tones over hearth fires.

"Don't be like that village in the west," people will say. "Not unless you want everyone you've ever loved to end up as ash."

My stomach heaves, and I glare at him. "But why bother with me at all?" I ask. "You've already got your witch. Why do you need two of us?"

He shrugs and takes a step back. "We don't need two," he says. "We only need you."

This sends a sharp jolt through me. "And Sara? What will you do with her?"

He smirks. "Whatever we want."

So much for all her loyalty to these men. I search the street for Sara, wanting to warn her, but she's already gone, and it chills me to think of where they've taken her.

A clutch of grumbling witchfinders hovers behind us as the doyen leads me through the town square where there are even more pyres, so many that it's dizzying. I don't want to follow him, but I have to stay close for now. I need him to take me to Anna and Beatrix. I need to help them. I won't watch them die too, turned to ash like my parents, like me probably before the night is over.

We pass the blacksmith's shop, the door barely ajar, and there's movement there on the other side. I hesitate, gazing inside, but the figure vanishes, and the witchfinders prod me on with the butts of their knives.

"No dragging your feet," they say, scoffing, and I bare my teeth at them before turning again to the doyen.

"Why are you doing any of this?" I ask. "What good can I possibly do for you that Sara can't?"

"Everything," he says and smiles. "One touch from you, and we won't need to light the fires. We'll have you do the honors."

At this, he lets out a hideous cackle, and my heart in my throat, I'm starting to understand them now. They want me as a show of force. It will be so much more terrifying for the witches they execute if another witch's touch is what sets them alight. I'll become these men's murder weapon, my body no different than a loop of rope or a pile of wilted straw. I'll belong to them.

Halting in the street, I tip my head up and look straight at him. "I'll die first," I say.

The doyen beams at me. "Will you though?" He inspects me up and down, his gaze heavier than a hundred hands. "Are you even sure you can die?"

"I guess we'll find out."

"Not quite yet." He waves one hand at me. "I have something else for you first."

I seize up, already knowing what it is.

"Anna and Beatrix." I can barely breathe now. "Where are they? What did you do with them?"

"Come with me," he says and motions me down the road. "I'll show you."

We find them at the stable, their hands tied behind their backs, their mouths gagged with ragged handkerchiefs, the witchfinders flanking them around a pair of horse troughs. I try to move toward them, but the men block my way, and there are more of them than I can imagine. Dozens, blotting the landscape worse than a cancer, and I think for a moment how cruel it is that they've brought Anna back home just to murder her.

"What are you doing with them?" I ask the doyen.

He tips his hat and wipes the sweat from his brow. "You know exactly what we're doing," he says, "We've got to test Anna and Beatrix first. Make sure they're heretics like you."

I exhale a strangled moan. Swimming the witches. That's why they're here. We don't have a river like in the capital, so these horse troughs will have to suffice.

At the edge of the fence, a group of witchfinders hold back a sobbing Samuel who looks so much smaller than I ever remember him. Farther out in the corral, the horses have been pushed to the periphery, their heads down, strangers now in their own terrain. Thanks to the doyen, we're all strangers here.

I surge forward again, but men surround me, quicker than I'll ever be, and the other witchfinders take hold of Beatrix and Anna. Grinning, they shove them into the troughs, filthy water burbling up and filling their lungs like the cruelest lullaby. I keep pushing forward, desperate to stop this, desperate to get to them, but the men close ranks tighter around me, pushing me to the ground where I'm easier to hold down. Screeching to the sky, I put my hands on their feet, their ankles, their thighs, anything to make them move, but they just press their boots deeper into my throat until I can't even manage a gasp.

My vision swimming at the edges, I turn and see Sara, standing back from the rest. Her hair in her face, her hands over her mouth, she gags out a whimper. Maybe she doesn't have the stomach for this after all.

The men yank Beatrix and Anna out of the water just for a moment, just long enough for them to catch their breath. Then they push them under all over again.

I thrash in the dirt, but the boots push harder into my body, and I cringe, my fingers clenching into fists. My hands are still numb, this magic weak and useless inside me. I've pushed down who I am for so long, made so many concessions to this village, to my mother, even to these men, that now when I need these spells, they're lost to me.

The doyen motions to the men. "Enough for now," he says, and the witchfinders back away, releasing Anna and Beatrix, releasing me too. I wheeze up a sob as the doyen drifts closer, that hideous face looming over me.

"This could take all night," he whispers. "Maybe I'll even stretch it out for days. If that's what you want."

I grit my teeth. "You know it isn't what I want."

"Then do something about it," he says. "Call it off, Odette. Right now. Tell me to send these men home tonight, back to the capital. Far away where they won't come after you or anyone else here."

I swallow hard, choking down his words, these bargains we're expected to make with men we loathe. From the gray glint in his eyes, it's clear he wants more from me than just a new sort of weapon. He wants a doll, a puppet he can play with. I'm a novelty to him. That's why he likes me—because if I say yes, he can toy with me and prod me for as long as he'd like. And when he's done, he can dissect me like a frog and see what makes me tick.

I start to tell him no or maybe to tell him yes because I have to do something. I can't let Anna and Beatrix die like this, but there's a struggle at the fence and a cry that echoes off the lingering clouds. Samuel has broken free and is shoving between the other witchfinders to reach the doyen.

"This isn't right. This isn't what you promised," he stammers as the others catch up with him and pull him back again.

The doyen waves him off as if he's shooing away a gnat. "Nonsense," he says. "I never promise anything."

The witchfinders still surrounding him, Samuel collapses to his knees and lets out a wail, and I've never felt so sorry for him in my whole life. If only he'd known better. If only he'd realized you can't make deals with men like this, not when their words are as empty as their hearts.

That means I can't make deals with them either. They won't set Anna and Beatrix free. They'll never give up a woman they've marked for burning.

My hands start to shake, and at last, I feel it. The magic, the rage, rising up in me again. It's so slight, little sparks here and there, just enough.

But when I look up at all their faces, too many to count, fear settles in my guts because I can't imagine anything I'll do will be enough. Only days ago, I could barely finish one witchfinder. There's no way I can contend with this many.

Trying not to scream, I turn away toward the fence. All the horses watch me now as though waiting on a cue, as though they're just as eager as I am to go after these men. I stare back at them, thinking how I was able to speak to them before and how maybe I can do it one more time.

At the troughs, the witchfinders grab Anna and Beatrix again, ready to baptize them in grime, and I lean forward, the palfrey I rode to the capital pushing to the front. I smile at him.

"Do whatever you please to them," I whisper, and with a grunt, the horses more than oblige. They charge forward, rearing up all around the men, and eyes wild, they bring down their hooves wherever they land. On boots, on backs, on bones that break in two, splintering like last spring's deadfall.

The witchfinders screech, their bodies twisting this way and that, chaos erupting all over the stable. Cutting between the men, I rush toward Anna and Beatrix, yanking the handkerchiefs out of their mouths, tugging at the knots on their hands, always careful not to let my skin touch theirs. The magic is slowly simmering inside me, everything about to boil over, and when a witchfinder charges toward us, I shove one hand at him, no more than a flick of the wrist, but it's enough to brand his face forever, his howls splitting the sky. I shudder to myself. I don't like what this is doing to me, how I'm seething with rage—the same as these men.

Samuel's fighting off the witchfinders too, punching and scratching and spitting at whoever's closest to him. He sees me lead Anna and Beatrix away, and he calls after his daughter, but we run from the stable and back toward the village with all its pyres.

On the cobblestone street, I expect we'll be alone, everyone cowering inside their homes, praying the witchfinders away, but I'm wrong. There's a line of women up ahead in the road. I count four of them starting toward us from the blacksmith's shop, and when we get closer, my breath catches in my chest because I recognize them.

They're all wearing my face.

A glamour. The women have conjured a glamour.

Three of them dodge to different parts of the street, whistling and waving at the witchfinders who are hollering behind us, but the *me* on the end breaks away and bids me to follow.

"This way," she whispers, and for a moment, I hesitate, not entirely convinced I should trust myself. But the men's shrieks dig into my back, and I'll do anything to escape them, so without a word, I rush toward the nearby alley where she's leading me. Anna and Beatrix follow, and together, we cluster close to the building, tucked back in a shadow as the witchfinders pass. Splitting up in the street, a group of them head toward each version of me.

When they've gone by, I turn and stare at my own face, and she looks back at me, flashing that crooked smile so familiar that it aches in my heart.

Freya. She never left after all. She stayed behind in this village she loathed, and I can already guess what she's been doing. Asking the girls I used to know for help, reminding them of the magic I once taught them. They're the ones scattered in the street now, leading the witchfinders in every direction, leading them away from me.

"You have to go now," Freya says and presses a small satchel into my pocket. "We'll stay back and hold them off."

My throat constricts. "How? I can't get past them."

"Sure, you can," she whispers. "Just be me."

Instantly I know what she means. I nod back at her, and my hands burning, I draw up this iota of magic within me, allowing it to settle over me like a thick cloak. When I'm done, I'm wearing my sister's face, and she's wearing mine, and we both need to run from each other all over again like we always do. No matter how hard we try, Freya and I are never heading in the same direction.

My sister reaches out for me, and with everything in me, I want to take her hand. I want to hold her close, but I know it isn't safe, so I just shake my head.

She smiles at me again anyhow. "See you soon, Odette," she whispers, and with a sharp laugh, Freya takes off into the street.

I want to go after her, but my chest heavy, I guide Beatrix and Anna the other way through backyards where we're not welcome and past storefronts boarded up tight. Breathless, we turn the corner at the general store, its copper roof glinting in the last sunlight of the day, but once we see what's on the other side, we jump back. Their sweat heavy and rank, the witchfinders are clogging up the main road out of town. They haven't spotted me, not yet, or if they have, they don't realize it. Their hateful eyes are searching for my face, not my sister's.

"Come on," I whisper and lead Beatrix and Anna down another alley, past the cinders of the house where I grew up and along the cobblestone street, the pyres marking our way like macabre signposts.

The three of us are headed the only way we can now—down the narrow dirt path out of town and toward the graveyard.

Passing through the rickety gates, we tiptoe around the crumbling mausoleums and dusty tombstones, careful not to step on any of the witches' graves, careful not to make much of a sound at all.

Not that being quiet ever helps. There's a creak of wagon wheels somewhere nearby, and my head jolts, waiting to hear it again, waiting for it to get closer, so I'll know which way to run. Everywhere we turn, there's someone or something that wants us.

No, that's not quite it. It's not *us* that's the problem. It's me.

I gaze at Beatrix and Anna, shivering next to me. Thanks to the witchfinders, their clothes are soaked though. In the February chill, neither one of them will last long like this, frostbite numbing their fingers, pneumonia sneaking into their lungs.

"The two of you should hide," I say. "Inside the mausoleum. It's not much, but you can wait this out."

Anna gapes at me. "We're not leaving you, Odette."

"Please," I say, my voice splitting in two. "I can't expect you to stay out here like this."

Beatrix chirps up a thin laugh. "Come now, darling," she says. "We don't have time for this foolishness."

A rattle at the cemetery gates, and my whole body goes numb because Beatrix is right: we don't have time. Their sharp voices calling out, the witchfinders materialize at the edge of the graveyard, their figures blazing in the sunset. They must have seen us escape the village and head this direction. Either that or they just know this is a place you can always find me.

I stumble backward, the three of us moving toward the fence, our feet tangled, and we try to hoist ourselves over. The men are closer now, and I'm sure it's too late, but then the ground shivers around us. I hold perfectly still, and Beatrix and Anna do the same, but the witchfinders pay no attention. They just keep coming, crossing the witches' graves like they're nothing. Another shudder in the dirt, and that's it—all at once, the men slip into the earth, one by one, their legs are buckling beneath them, the graves swallowing them whole.

At first, I think it's a spell, something I'm conjuring or maybe something Freya's done. But as the men keep collapsing into the ground, barely able to fight their way back up again, I realize it's not a spell at all. It's because all the graves are empty, all thanks to me. Those nights I lost, the ones I couldn't remember—I was here, hollowing out the earth. I've dug up the dead, more bones than I can count, and now nobody is left behind, certainly not the witches these men executed.

Anna whimpers, cradling herself. "Where have all the bodies gone?" she asks, her voice rasping, and something tenses deep inside me, my eyes shifting toward the woods, past the burning trees and deeper into the darkness.

The Hyland Forest. It's been calling to me for years. I must have answered it more times than I ever realized. That's where the bones are, where I've directed the children to bury them. And it's the only place left for us to go.

I finish pulling myself to the other side of the fence, and Beatrix and Anna follow.

"This way," I say, and we head toward what's left of the forest.

At the crossroads, the little girl is waiting there with the other children.

"We're coming too, Odette," she says. "We don't want to miss the end of the game."

She grins, so close she can almost reach out and touch us as the children pull the wagon behind her, filled with the last of the bones. My crow is there too. His eyes are open now, watching my every move. They'll follow me up into the forest the same way they have before, and they're not the only ones tracking us. The men are venturing after us too. The woods aren't verboten to them now. That's because they've got a witch to guide them. Sara, her fury burning almost as bright as their torches. She might not have had the stomach to watch the men torturing Anna and Beatrix, but she'll be more than happy to do the same thing to me.

I won't think of it now. I just keep going. The three of us snake our way through smoldering trees until we reach it. This one slice of land that hasn't burned, its skin as impervious to fire as mine. When we slip through the border into the Hyland Forest, it's immediately summer again, the air hanging heavy with the sticky scent of honeysuckle. Anna and Beatrix huddle together, no longer shivering, and wring the gray water out of their clothes. Standing next to them, my breath heaving, the glamour shatters around me, and here I am, once again wearing my own face.

My fingers still shaking, the magic coiling tighter within me, I reach into my pocket and remove the satchel my sister gave me. It's filled with salt. Of course, it is. Freya, always knowing how to outsmart trouble. It's almost dark now, and she knew I'd need this. I close my eyes and envision her back in the village. She's still alive and so are the other girls I used to know. They're heading toward the forest too, a snarl of witchfinders close behind them. I tell myself they'll make it, my sister will make it, but I wonder if that's true.

My fingers burn, and I can feel it rising up in me again. This power, almost too much for me to bear.

The sun dipping in the sky, I pour a circle of salt around us. The phantoms are already here, pinwheeling and screeching and creeping closer, and they're not only in the edges of my vision anymore. They're everywhere now, their gazes clear to me, and though I don't want to, though I'm safe inside the salt ring, I start to inch forward nearer to the darkness, nearer to this place where it feels like I belong. It's so natural to go toward them into the gloom that should have claimed me on the pyre.

But as I drift closer to the darkness, Anna moves toward me, her hand quivering near mine, ready to take hold of me even if it sears straight through her.

"Don't," she says. "Please, Odette. Stay here."

I look at her, that ruddy face I know so well, and I look at Beatrix too, still wearing that same sad smile.

"I wish I could," I whisper.

I wish so many things. For the last five years, I wish I could have stayed with them, the three of us together and stronger for it. I wish Freya would have been with us as well. We could have prepared ourselves for this day when the witchfinders would return. We could have been ready. But none of that matters now. The men are coming, and nothing will stop them. Nothing except me and these shadows swirling all around us.

When the witchfinders get here, they'll overtake me, but maybe the darkness can overtake them too. That might give Beatrix and Anna a chance. That might give everyone in the village a chance. I'll be gone, but maybe these men will be gone along with me.

I've tried all these years to keep the witchfinders out. Now I'll go to them instead.

With the gloom descending on me, I hold my breath and step out of the salt circle.

chapter thirteen

THE SHADOWS ENGULF ME IN AN INSTANT, AND THIS TIME, THEY DON'T LIFT me up and take me away. That's because they've already got me exactly where they want me, the place they've been leading me all along. They swirl up out of the dirt where they're buried, where the children and I buried them. This piece of earth belongs to these phantoms now, and their power is so much stronger here. Magic has always been stronger here.

Tears streak down my face, but there's nowhere I can go, not even back into the salt circle, not now. The ghosts are all around me, pressing closer, and they're so very hungry. I open my mouth to scream, and the shadows thread through me, taking my body as their own. They get into me any way they can, sneaking up arms and between my lips, leaking into every gap between my bones, puddling beneath my fingernails like malignant growths.

Wheezing, Anna and Beatrix start toward me, but I motion them back, my hand quivering and hardly my own, the darkness corkscrewing through me.

"Don't," I whisper. "Please."

Anna and Beatrix need to stay there in the salt circle. They need to stay safe.

I close my eyes, and somewhere deep in the earth, there's a faint melody, one I recognize at once. The birds' songs, disembodied and lost. This trick the woods have been using to lure me, this is why the birds have no voices. They're buried as deep as the bones of the dead.

I part my lips to call out to them, to try to give them back what they lost, but at the edge of the forest, Freya and the other girls appear, the glamour faded, their faces returned.

My stomach twists. "Run," I say, the ghosts settling deep in my belly, my bones, everywhere in me.

But there's nowhere left for them to go. With the witchfinders right behind them, they're trapped here with me and this gloom that's claimed me for its own. Nothing in my body feels like mine anymore. Within my flesh, there are more of these ghosts than there is of me. I'm an invader in my own skin.

Everything in me shaking, I reach into my pocket and toss Freya the satchel she gave me. "A circle," I say. "Make a circle."

The ground humming beneath us, alive and restless, they pour a careful ring around the four of them, my sister and these three girls I used to call friends. This will keep them safe. Just in time too.

There's only one shadow left now, rising up out of the ground, its figure gossamer, the scents of sandalwood and jasmine dancing in the air. My flesh tightens on my bones, and I can't take my eyes off this apparition. That's because I know her.

Freya gazes toward the figure too, her breath halting in her chest. "Mama?" she asks, her voice small and pitiful.

"Stay in the circle, Freya," I say, and I'd give anything to be able to take my sister's hand and pull her away from all this. "Don't get any closer."

But my sister was never very good at listening. She starts toward our mother, toward this unnerving shadow that towers over everything, and I start to scream, but it's already too late. With her spectral hand, our mother shoves Freya aside, just like she always did. I'm the one she wants, her marionette.

I try to back away, but she's too quick for me. Her form everywhere at once, she knocks me off my feet, and once I'm down, she looms over me, her shape gaunt and stretched and unreal. This shadow of hers is so familiar, the same one that's been following me all these nights, fogging up the windows and knocking at the doors.

"It's you. It's always been you," I murmur. Our mother, sending me on her midnight errands, making me dig up these ghosts for her. Anything to bring her power.

Near us, the children have arrived, and they're watching my mother and watching me too, the little girl's face pale and strained. They haven't tried to inhabit my body like the rest, which means they must not be ghosts after all. They're flesh and blood like us. Until this moment, I wasn't sure, but as the darkness swirls in me, the same way it must swirl in them, I'm starting to understand the rules the children have been playing by. The orphans of witches, they've been my mother's foot soldiers. Somewhere along the line, she became their own personal pied piper, leading them away from the villages that had forgotten them, whispering in their ears about how she could bring back their parents. All they needed to do was play a game with her. Then she'd give them back everything they lost: a family, a home, a life.

And hell, maybe she can bring their parents back, just not in the way the children want.

The other girls pull a half-dazed Freya back into the salt circle, and the Hyland Forest shudders around us. When the forest tried to draw me back into its embrace, this isn't what it had in mind. It wanted spells and secrets and birds rising up out of the earth. It never asked for this much death. Not that my mother cares. What remains of her face contorts, and it's so strange to see a shadow laugh.

There's a rustling at the border of the field. From every direction, the witchfinders push between the willows. Sneering to each other, they start to surround us, Samuel following behind them and still calling out for Anna.

"Please," I whisper to my mother. "We can stop this together."

I try to take her hand, to hold her close, but she only shakes her head. We both know she's never liked my way of doing things. A final laugh, like a tempest over the ocean, and my mother envelops me, seeping into every crevice of my body, inhabiting my bones. After all these years, she finally has the power she always wanted: mine.

I hold my breath, trying to fight this, trying to fend her off, but I can't stop it now. She's the reason this place tried to devour me before. There are more troubled ghosts in this world than you could ever fathom, and my mother's managed to find them all and bring them to me. I'm their vessel, a thousand souls restless within me, everything in my body not my own.

The witchfinders advance, the doyen and Sara commanding from the back, everyone headed right for me. They still think they're the most dangerous thing here, and because I know what's to come, it would be easy to feel sorry for them, but I don't. All I want is to free myself from this, to have my body back, but the ghosts have other plans. One by one, a hundred tendrils of thick smoke run out of me, never splitting my skin, never ripping me apart the way they should. These long waves of inky darkness twitch down along the dirt like heavy mist, following you no matter where you run. And the men certainly do run, especially once they realize they're outnumbered by something far stronger and stranger than them.

The willows sway all around us, and the Hyland Forest cries out, begging us to stop, but my mother pays it no mind. She's got what she wants now. It's a symphony of strident sounds, trembling through the ground. A splintering of bone here, a throat sliced by a nearly invisible hand there. Splashes of red array the patches of violets and dandelions sprouting from the earth, and the men fall one by one like a row of wooden dominoes.

The ghosts are drawing this from me, drawing out my own power, latent for so long I didn't even know it was this strong. But they knew—my mother's always known—and now they're using me however they please. I want to turn away, but wherever I look, I can still see the witchfinders, dying everywhere.

And they're not alone. Samuel's here too, trying to get to his daughter, crying out as a shadow yanks him down toward the earth, its spiny fingers viscous as tar, sticking to him. A thrash of his legs, and he breaks away for a moment, crawling on his belly, and Anna screams at him and at me, begging us to hide in the salt circle, begging us to come to her.

Samuel edges closer to her, the darkness tugging at him, and I wish I could go to them as well. But I can't breathe now. I'm not even sure I have lungs left to breathe. Within this cage of my bones, I can't be sure I have anything left of me at all, my insides turning liquid and useless.

I close my eyes again and feel the darkness moving beyond the Hyland Forest. Using me as an anchor, it's spiraling out in every direction. Toward our village, toward all the other villages, into the capital too. It's headed every place at once. From miles off, I can hear when the screaming starts. The darkness is leeching into everyone now, tightening their bones from within, killing them slowly and sweetly like a cruel caress.

My mother, vengeance boiling in what's left of her heart. I don't fault her for hating the witchfinders. I hate them too. We all do. But she's ready to burn the whole world to ash. She'll never run out of people to blame.

The villagers who cowered in their homes, sobbing and clutching their children, their shutters and doors locked tight while their neighbors burned.

The witches like my sister who ran and hid and tried to save themselves.

The fishmongers who sold the witchfinders their suppers, the scared girls at taverns who served them their wine, the widows who looked away at the public executions.

There will always be someone else my mother hasn't punished yet. She's never cared who she hurts, not even if it's her own daughters. If I let the shadows devour the witchfinders, they'll devour everything else too.

The little girl is crying now and so are all her friends, none of them so fearsome as before. As men die all around them, they're only scared children now, and for the first time, everyone can see them.

"Where did you come from?" the girls I used to know ask, but before they can break the circle, Freya holds them back. They're still safe, tucked away within the salt, the same as Beatrix and Anna.

And there's someone else doing the same thing. Beneath a drooping willow, Sara is hiding in her own circle, collapsed on her knees, sobbing into cupped hands, praying to the sky or the earth or anyone who will listen. This isn't what she wanted. It isn't what any of us wanted. Revenge never is, not really. You're always so sure it will fix everything, but mostly it just breaks something else.

Samuel's finally reached Anna's circle, and she gives him her hand to help him inside. But a darkness casts over our faces, and this time, it isn't from the ghosts. It's a witchfinder, standing over me. This man with a thin red cut on his cheek, the same man from the capital who tried to kill me once before.

"Now where were we?" he asks, gripping his knife a little tighter as he straddles me, his knees on either side of my body, never touching me. The darkness swirls around him, but he hardly seems to notice.

Turning away from me, Samuel starts to pull himself into the salt circle with Anna, but then he gazes into his daughter's face, twisted and weeping for me. Her arms reach out blindly, though she knows she can't get to me, and Samuel finally sees me as she does, as someone who's not the enemy he always thought I was.

He hesitates before reaching out and squeezing his daughter's hand. "It's all right," he whispers to her, and gathering himself to his feet, he slips the secret dagger out of his boot. As the witchfinder raises his blade to me, Samuel sneaks up from behind and does the same to him. I inhale, my skin crawling and contorting as though I'm being flayed alive, and in an instant, Samuel slashes the witchfinder's throat. It's just a quick motion, and I think how much easier this all could have been had he done the same thing to his nephew only a few days ago.

But he's done this now. After everything, he's saved me. Samuel wipes the blade on his trousers and extends his hand toward me, forgetting he can't touch me, forgetting that I'm fire. But before I can utter a word, Anna screams out, and with a final breath, the bleeding witchfinder turns and buries the blade meant for me in Samuel's chest instead.

For a bottomless moment, Samuel gazes at me, his eyes fading, and I stare back at him, wishing I could move, wishing I could do anything at all.

"Finish this, Odette," he says, a ribbon of blood leaking from his lips before his whole body crumples next to me. Anna lets out a wail that could split the sky, and Beatrix pulls her close, shielding her face from her father's body.

Nearby, someone exhales a laugh, shrill and cruel. "Look what you've done now, Odette."

The doyen. No more than a dozen paces away, he's cast his own circle. His men are dying all around him, but he doesn't seem to notice. Everyone is expendable to him.

Blood on the earth at their feet, the little girl and the rest of the children are weeping louder now, and the schoolteacher can't bear it any longer. She rushes to them, but the darkness rushes to her as well, its thin fingers yanking her to the ground and raking across her skin. She cries out, and Freya and the other girls break the circle to help her just as the shadows seize them as well. They fight off the gloom better than the witchfinders, their magic still sizzling within them. But it won't be enough.

I thrash against the earth, but the ghosts hold me down, pinning my bones into the dirt as they loop around every throat they can find. The distant screams in the villages are becoming muffled, and soon there will be no one left to cry.

I look to Anna, wishing I could call her name. Her throat raw from sobbing, she looks back at me, and her eyes turn to steel, a resolve budding inside her. She leans down, and with a careful hand, she gathers the salt from her circle, breaking the barrier. The eager ghosts descend on her now but not before she casts the salt toward me, a thin line along my body.

Already the shadows are braiding around her, blistering her skin, but the other girls have seen what she's done. They drag themselves across the earth on their bellies, the phantoms still coiled around them like thick snakes, and they scoop up bits of salt from their circle. Their fingers shaking, they cast it toward me. One after another, they take handfuls from the earth and give them to me. It's a small ring, but it will be enough. If they can close it, it could stop all of this.

The willows whisper all around us, and still safe in her own circle, Sara watches, understanding what the other girls are doing. How they're trying to seal away the darkness.

With Beatrix helping her, Freya pours the last handful of salt they can gather, but it isn't enough. The circle still isn't closed.

"I'm sorry, Odette," Freya whispers, collapsed and curled up on the ground next to me, the gloom tightening around her throat. The shadows are draping over all of them now, oppressive as a funeral shroud.

My body paralyzed, I search the forest wildly, and Sara gazes back at me. Just like in the capital, something passes between us. This spark, this understanding. From one witch to another. She swallows a sob because she knows what to do even though she doesn't want to. Her body shaking, she gathers up as much salt as she can hold, breaking her own ring of protection, and she moves toward me. With the shadows weaving around her, lashing at her throat, she casts the final handful of salt, completing the circle.

At once, the shadows are cut off, the inky tendrils withdrawing from everywhere: the capital, the villages, the girls' bodies. But it's different this time. The salt hasn't sealed the phantoms out. Because they're all writhing within me, it's sealed them in. I'm alone with this darkness. With my mother.

Although the shadows have let them go, Freya and the other girls are still struggling against the earth, their bodies weak and bruised. Beatrix can barely move, and Anna is crouched on her knees, her wails piercing the sky. The Hyland Forest murmurs to them, trying to help them to their feet, but I look past them all to someone who's still standing.

The doyen. He's been safe in his own salt ring this whole time. Now he breaches the barrier, and taking a few final steps, he lingers at the edge of my circle.

Curled in the dirt, I'm too weak to move or run or even spit at him.

He moves nearer to me. "I'm so sorry this has to end so soon," he says, his boots still on the outside of the salt, "but you've become too much of a nuisance, Odette."

The stench of his sweat hanging heavy in the air, he removes his flint and iron from his pocket, wetting his lips slowly like he'd give anything to use his mouth on me just once before he finishes me.

Quivering with glee, he's ready to set me alight all over again. His hand can strike this flame and let it fall on me in this circle. That way, he never has to touch me, never has to risk himself.

I grit my teeth and steady myself. The ghosts whisper within me, my mother shifting in my bones, desperate to crack me in two from the inside, but what they don't understand is we're together in this circle, trapped as one. So long as the salt is around us, they can no longer draw up what's inside me and use it against the world. They thought I was at their mercy, but with nowhere for them to go now, it's me they can't escape. This moment, this chance to use my power the way I want instead of the way I'm told.

My lips dry, I exhale a whistle, sweet and sharp. Just once, and it's more than enough.

The sky clouds over, and the doyen hesitates. "An eclipse?" he asks, gazing upward, and I smile.

"Not today," I say.

All the birds are here, blotting out the sky. They've come back for me with a familiar shape leading the way. My crow. He's broken his tether on the children's wagon, and he circles overhead with the rest, awaiting my cue.

At my cottage, I wouldn't do a spell to chain him to me even though I wanted him to stay. But maybe now I can do something else. With all this power brimming within me, I can give him back what he lost, what all the birds lost.

I part my lips again and draw up the melody the Hyland Forest stole. It flows through my bones, and I let the birds take this from me, pulling it up out of my throat, tearing it away from these ghosts that occupy me.

All the birds swallow it down, circling closer to us now. With my crow at the helm, they tip back their heads to the sky and exhale a single note, their voices so sweet and clear they make me want to weep and scream at the same time.

The phantoms twist within me, writhing and cursing, but the birds' melodies only grow louder. They just keep singing, and even the doyen grimaces and plugs his ears. This beautiful dirge that terrorizes the dead and the deathmongers alike.

My mother twitches inside me, and she guides my hand toward the circle, ready to wipe the salt away, to free herself again.

But with the birds still singing, I clench my fingers into a fist and hold her back. "You don't get to choose anymore," I whisper.

This is all a spell. Everything from the fire in my bones to the dead dancing from their graves. And it's a rule my mother taught me when I was young: so long as there's a breath left in you, you can always break a spell.

I'll shatter what these men have done. What my mother's done too.

Wincing away from the birds, the doyen inches closer, almost inside the circle now, and he raises his iron and flint over me, still smirking, always smirking. But this time, I smirk back, and I reach up and seize him by the wrists, wrapping my fingers around him tighter than a hangman's knot.

And I don't let go.

It flows out of me slowly at first as though after all these years it's not in any hurry at all. His eyes widening, his flesh blistering, the doyen flails against me, but even as his hands fumble, desperate to strike the iron and flint, the flames rush out of me faster, returning to him at last, this man who set our world alight.

I wrench him the rest of the way into the circle, and a thin border of fire rises up from the salt, the same way as when I conjured the spell in the capital. Trapped in here with me, the doyen can't escape now. The flint slipping from his hands, I keep holding onto him, and this is more than before, more than a simple touch. The fire scorches through me, hurting so much worse than I expect. It might turn me to nothing too, but I don't care. This is the only way. After everything, this is the right way.

Their shrieks sharp as briars, the ghosts inside me splinter apart, and my mother's voice echoes in my bones along with the other voices of the dead. They don't want this spell to end. They want it to go on forever.

But I smile because they won't get their way this time. I empty everything I have into the doyen. All these phantoms, this fire, this pain I refused to forget.

He pulls me closer one last time, everything in him bristling and unrepentant. "I'll finish you," he murmurs, the words dissolving on his lips as everything else in him dissolves too. His body is filling up with heat, but I don't take my hands off him—not when his flesh turns to ash, not even when the ash turns to dust, glimmering like distant stars in the night.

I only let him go once there's nothing left to hold.

His glittering remains lilt to the sky, and the birds pluck pieces of him from the air, swallowing him down before retching him back up again. They don't want him lingering in their bellies.

I pull myself up to my feet, and I hesitate, hollowed-out from what I lost. I feel empty now, but I feel new and whole too. With a steady hand, I wipe away the salt circle and step out into a night that has no phantoms left to haunt me.

Freya watches me, her eyes dark, her body still weak. "Are you all right?" she asks, and I nod just as the sky tilts, and the whole world fades to gray around me.

chapter fourteen

When I open my eyes, I'm still curled up in the forest, and I'm sure I must be dead. All those ghosts stretched my insides like taffy, and it must have killed me.

I roll over onto my back, everything in me heavy and sore. Out of nowhere, the little girl leans over me, her eyes wide, and I blink up at her.

"Am I dead yet?" I ask.

She laughs. "No, silly," she says, and I squint up into the sun. That's when I see Freya, sitting cross-legged next to me.

"Welcome back," she says, smiling.

My body numb, I struggle to sit up in the dirt. "Why are we still here?"

"Because," she says, "Beatrix said this was the best place for you to get well."

A witch convalescing in the woods. Beatrix would like that.

I sink deeper into the ground, and sensation leaks back into my body, a little bit at a time. The ache in my bones. The stinging of my eyes. Someone holding my hand.

Freya. My sister is holding my hand.

I try to wrench away from her, to keep my flesh from searing through hers, but she only shakes her head.

"It's all right," she whispers, our fingers still entwined. "You're all right now."

I stare down at my own skin, marveling at a body that finally belongs to me again. No longer burning inside me, the flames from the pyres have gone at last. In spite of himself, the doyen finally extinguished them.

The little girl gives me that gap-toothed grin. "Look at that," she says. "You've won the game, Odette."

She and the other children skip in a circle around me, humming their strange songs, their faces clear to me now, all the ghosts leeched out of them, just as they no longer live in me.

Freya laughs and watches them as I tighten my fingers around her hand. It's been so long since I've been this close to my sister, this close to anyone.

I gaze up, and my crow is nestled in a nearby willow along with a dozen other birds, cardinals and blue jays and wrens, all of them watching over me like patient midwives.

This forest is so different from how I left it last night. It's quieter now and cleaner too. There are no bodies left behind. My heart heaves in my chest because I know where they've gone. The earth must have cracked in two and swallowed down the decay, consuming all the things we didn't want to look at anymore.

I breathe deep. "Are all of the men dead?"

Freya hesitates. "Most of them," she says. "The rest ran off into the night. We haven't seen them since."

If only we could never see them again.

I manage to sit up, and the ground whispers *good morning* to me. The Hyland Forest is blossoming everywhere, a ring of chrysanthemums and daffodils turning their blooms toward me, the earth cradling my body until I'm well again, nursing me back to health. This is the land's way of saying thank you—for returning and setting it free of my mother and her phantoms. The forest saved me because I helped to save it.

Only I wasn't alone. My sister was here and so were the girls I thought had forgotten me, the friends my mother warned me about. We were together in this.

And someone else was with us too. Sara. She's still here, helping Anna and Beatrix now, and they're bringing me a poultice made from the lavender they've gathered beneath a patch of willows.

When she sees I'm awake, Sara recoils. "Are you going to finish me too?" she asks, her hair curtaining her eyes. "Like you did the doyen?"

We watch each other for a long moment, the ground murmuring beneath me, the birds chattering in the trees. I want to hate her. It would be so easy to do, to remind myself why she deserves it. Her betrayal, her vengeance, her cowardice. I could justify it a hundred different ways. Just like my mother justified what she did to me.

I shake my head. "No," I say at last.

There's been enough death. Enough burned bodies and mangled bone to last a hundred lifetimes. We have a chance to change this path, to make this moment different than all the ones that came before.

A sprig of lavender in her hair, Anna leans down and takes my other hand.

I can barely look at her. "I'm so sorry about Samuel," I whisper, and she nods.

"I know," she says, and Beatrix presses the poultice across my forehead, extracting the last of the sickness from my body.

Everything is changing. From faraway, I can feel it. All the villagers and all the witches in the capital too. They're still with us. The darkness didn't unravel them the way it wanted to. The shadows tried to devour them, but I drew the ghosts back before it was too late.

And now in all those villages, they know what we've done. They can feel it too. This power, this magic. They want a taste of it themselves. That way, the next time men like the doyen descend on us, they will know how to fight back too.

"They're coming to us," I say and look to the sky where my crow sings an elegy back at me.

They arrive one after another and always at dusk.

The woman from behind the counter of the apothecary. The girl I freed in the Wharf District. Those who have been conjuring for a lifetime, and those who can't even imagine a simple glamour.

They sneak up into the woods as though they aren't welcome. They don't understand yet that this land thrives on magic. And when they emerge at the edge of the willows where I once cracked the reflection, we're already waiting for them, eager for them to join us. Because with each new arrival, the Hyland Forest is coming alive again in the way I remember it, the way it was when we were young.

And not everyone comes from far-off places. The girls I used to know are here as well. They've brought their daughters and their sons too.

The clerk from the general store, the blacksmith's wife, the schoolteacher. Rosalind, Isabelle, Cecily. I remember their names now. I remember everything, all the nights we called out to the moon, all the spells I tried to forget.

I'm not alone. I'll never be alone again. That's what my mother couldn't understand. We have to share this burden. It's the only way to fight men like the doyen.

As Anna and Sara greet another wanderer into the woods, I gaze through the thin bones of what's left of the ashen forest, and from miles away, I can see it. Backlit against the empty sky, my cottage is a skeleton of ash, seared right down to the foundation. After what the witchfinders have done, it won't ever be the same.

On the wind, spectral voices still lilt all around me, the bones buried in the earth but not so restless as before. I feel them everywhere, a whisper in the trees, a thick rustling in the grass. Our mother's here too and so is our father, and I say goodbye to them because for the first time they're free. All the ghosts are free. The spell is broken, and the dead no longer hold sovereignty over me.

Of course, there are those who aren't dead at all. Not all the witchfinders were turned to dust. Maybe they'll run forever after what they witnessed, or maybe they'll be back in a fortnight, a grudge in their heart, iron and flint in their pocket. Or it could always be different men next time, the sons and nephews and grandchildren of the ones who came before. After all, the world is made for witchfinders. One way or another, we'll fight against them forever. But if we're together, maybe we'll be ready for them this time.

Until then, Anna and Sara toss their heads back and laugh, both of them dancing with the giggling children and the newcomers, all their bare feet quivering and rising off the earth.

I laugh too and then I turn away from them.

I want to tell myself all the darkness is gone, but there's a well inside me where the flames used to be. A hollowness that's wider and more unforgiving than the universe. I haven't figured out yet how to fill it. When you've held onto pain for this long, you feel so empty when it's gone.

Beatrix kneels next to me and places a sun-spotted hand over mine. "Try not to worry, Odette," she says, and I rest my head in the crook of her arm. "This storm won't last forever."

Overhead, my crow darts back and forth, mingling with a starling and a magpie and a dove, the living and the departed scattered across the sky until you can't tell one from the other. All of the birds have returned, the ghosts that have guided me and the others that fled long ago. The enchantment runs wild now, just the way it always should have.

And the enchantment is just getting started. Restless as always, Freya has gone off to bring back all the witches she can find, inviting them out of the hidden alcoves and tucked-away cottages where they've been hiding these long years. She's on her way home now, and when I close my eyes, I see all of them on the road. They'll be here soon, and we're so eager to welcome them because there's so much for us to learn. For me to learn as well. After all the times I tried to teach others, now I'll be able to sit back and listen too. There are so many spells I can't even fathom. We can share this now. We can share everything.

When Freya arrives, all of us will gather together, nestling in the grass, the forest whispering its secrets to us. Still giggling, the children will join us too, their faces clear, their eyes bright.

"Is this a new game?" the little girl will ask, and I'll nod.

With everyone ready for what comes next, I'll settle down in the dirt with them, and Anna and Beatrix will sit next to me, and without hesitating, they'll wrap their hands around mine. I'll smile and hold onto them a little tighter. Then I'll look to all the waiting faces around me.

"Let us begin," I'll say, and all the birds will sing in tune.

Gwendolyn Kiste is the Bram Stoker Award–winning author of *The Rust Maidens* from Trepidatio Publishing; *And Her Smile Will Untether the Universe* from JournalStone; and the dark fantasy novella *Pretty Marys All in a Row* from Broken Eye Books. Her short fiction has appeared in *Nightmare Magazine*, Nightfire's *Come Join Us by the Fire*, *Black Static*, *Daily Science Fiction*, *Shimmer*, *Interzone*, and *LampLight*, among others. Originally from Ohio, she now resides on an abandoned horse farm outside of Pittsburgh with her husband, two cats, and not nearly enough ghosts. Find her online at gwendolynkiste.com.

BROKEN EYE BOOKS

Sign up for our newsletter at
www.brokeneyebooks.com

Welcome to Broken Eye Books! Our goal is to bring you the weird and funky, the stories you just can't get anywhere else. We want to create books that blend genres and break expectations, stories with fascinating characters and forward-thinking ideas. We want to keep exploring and celebrating the joy of storytelling.

If you want to help us and all the authors and artists involved in our projects, please leave a review for this book! Every single review will help this title get noticed by someone who might not have seen it otherwise.

And stay tuned because we've got more coming . . .

OUR BOOKS

The Hole Behind Midnight, by Clinton J. Boomer
Crooked, by Richard Pett
Scourge of the Realm, by Erik Scott de Bie
Izanami's Choice, by Adam Heine
Pretty Marys All in a Row, by Gwendolyn Kiste
Queen of No Tomorrows, by Matt Maxwell
The Great Faerie Strike, by Spencer Ellsworth
Catfish Lullaby, by A.C. Wise
Busted Synapses, by Erica L. Satifka
Boneset & Feathers, by Gwendolyn Kiste

COLLECTIONS

Royden Poole's Field Guide to the 25th Hour, by Clinton J. Boomer
Team Murderhobo: Assemble, by Clinton J. Boomer

ANTHOLOGIES

(edited by Scott Gable & C. Dombrowski)

By Faerie Light: Tales of the Fair Folk

Ghost in the Cogs: Steam-Powered Ghost Stories

Tomorrow's Cthulhu: Stories at the Dawn of Posthumanity

Ride the Star Wind: Cthulhu, Space Opera, and the Cosmic Weird

Welcome to Miskatonic University: Fantastically Weird Tales of Campus Life

It Came from Miskatonic University: Weirdly Fantastical Tales of Campus Life

Nowhereville: Weird Is Other People

Cooties Shot Required: There Are Things You Must Know

Whether Change: The Revolution Will Be Weird

Stay weird.

Read books.

Repeat.

brokeneyebooks.com

twitter.com/brokeneyebooks

facebook.com/brokeneyebooks

instagram.com/brokeneyebooks

patreon.com/brokeneyebooks

CPSIA information can be obtained
at www.ICGtesting.com
Printed in the USA
LVHW051518201020
669305LV00004B/936